SAVAGE
THE STAMPEDERS

SAVAGE TEXAS
THE STAMPEDERS

William W. Johnstone
with J. A. Johnstone

PINNACLE BOOKS
Kensington Publishing Corp.
www.kensingtonbooks.com

PINNACLE BOOKS are published by

Kensington Publishing Corp.
119 West 40th Street
New York, NY 10018

Copyright © 2013 J. A. Johnstone

All rights reserved. No part of this book may be reproduced in any form or by any means without the prior written consent of the publisher, excepting brief quotes used in reviews.

PUBLISHER'S NOTE
Following the death of William W. Johnstone, the Johnstone family is working with a carefully selected writer to organize and complete Mr. Johnstone's outlines and many unfinished manuscripts to create additional novels in all of his series like The Last Gunfighter, Mountain Man, and Eagles, among others. This novel was inspired by Mr. Johnstone's superb storytelling.

If you purchased this book without a cover, you should be aware that this book is stolen property. It was reported as "unsold and destroyed" to the publisher, and neither the author nor the publisher has received any payment for this "stripped book."

All Kensington titles, imprints, and distributed lines are available at special quantity discounts for bulk purchases for sales promotions, premiums, fund-raising, educational, or institutional use. Special book excerpts or customized printings can also be created to fit specific needs. For details, write or phone the office of the Kensington special sales manager: Kensington Publishing Corp., 119 West 40th Street, New York, NY 10018, attn: Special Sales Department; phone 1-800-221-2647.

PINNACLE BOOKS and the Pinnacle logo are Reg. U.S. Pat. & TM Off.
The WWJ steer head logo is a trademark of Kensington Publishing Corp.

ISBN-13: 978-0-7860-3136-8
ISBN-10: 0-7860-3136-0

First printing: November 2013

10 9 8 7 6 5 4 3 2 1

Printed in the United States of America

First electronic edition: November 2013

ISBN-13: 978-0-7860-3137-5
ISBN-10: 0-7860-3137-9

PROLOGUE

The annals of the Old West tell of fateful alliances between lawmen and outlaws, some of the most notable being those of Wyatt Earp and Doc Holliday, Pat Garrett and Billy the Kid, and Bat Masterson and Ben Thompson.

To these legendary team-ups must be added the names of Sam Heller and Johnny Cross, whose on-again, off-again deadly friendship proves instrumental in shaping the destiny of the folk of Hangtree County, Texas, and ultimately the history of the Southwest.

Sam Heller is a Yankee, a Kansas man who tries to live by the precepts of the Bible and the law but by doing so often finds himself on the wrong side of evildoers cloaked in the guise of authority.

Johnny Cross is an outlaw and gunfighter who professes to believe only in his own raw nerve and lightning-fast draw, yet whose sense of fair play more often than not finds him fighting on the side of the angels.

The common thread binding these two unlikely allies is a Texas town called Hangtree, a lonely outpost on the edge of civilization that will battle the forces of savagery and destruction to become a cattle country empire in the county that bears its name.

The settlement is located on the Pecos River near the West Texas border, south of the sprawling Staked Plains region. It takes its name from a lone, lofty, lightning-blasted oak that served as a gallows for a gang of renegade deserters during the Mexican-American War who terrorized the region until decent folk fed up with their depredations banded together to eliminate the outlaws by stringing them up from the tree. The tree still stands as a symbol of justice in a lawless land.

Our saga begins in 1866. The Civil War is over. Like other states in what had been the Confederacy, Texas is in dire straits.

Most of the men have been away for years, fighting since the war began. Many are now dead and will not return; a number of the survivors are missing limbs or are otherwise seriously wounded. Even those who return whole and intact possess little more than the clothes on their backs and the muskets they've been allowed to keep during the demobilization.

Their long absence has worked great hardship

on the families they left behind. Homes have been pillaged and burned, farmlands have returned to wilderness, remnants of cattle herds have wandered off into the brush. Displaced kinfolk have been scattered to the four winds.

Little peace and less justice awaits the returnees, with Texas hard-pressed under the yoke of the Governor Davis administration. Davis and his corrupt minions, a ring of homegrown scalawags and outland carpetbaggers, plunder all they can, protected by federal occupation troops whose primary mission is to keep the ex-rebels down.

Outlaw bands ravage the state at will, while the central and western regions are also prey to Comanche raiders grown strong while peacekeeping efforts languished during the war years.

But despite the hardships life goes on and the slow, shaky business of rebuilding begins.

The town called Hangtree has been hard-hit by the neglect of the war years, but its location along a key gateway trail to the southwest, and its well-watered grazing lands, have kept it alive, a patch of civilization in a howling wilderness.

Several square blocks of wooden frame buildings stand at the crossroads, ringed by a scattering of tumbledown ranches and farms. It seems little more than a ghost town, but Hangtree is already beginning to quicken with renewed life and commerce. War's end has loosed hordes of ex-soldiers and civilians migrating to the open lands, mineral deposits, opportunity, and freedom from oppressive government in the Southwest.

The hollows and thickets of the grasslands surrounding Hangtree teem with maverick cattle belonging to anyone who can put their brand on them, round them up, and bring them to market.

Instrumental to the town's prospects is its nearness (a day's ride away, a short distance in the Lone Star state) to Fort Price, a U.S. cavalry outpost newly remanned to deter Comanche war parties raiding their way south through Texas and into Mexico. But the cavalry is not only a potential savior but also a threat to the citizenry, due to their officers being charged to support the venal Governor Davis administration.

To Hangtree comes Sam Heller, an ex-captain who was one of the best rifle shots in the Union army and a veteran of many dangerous behind-the-lines missions for Allan Pinkerton's Secret Service during the war. His wanderings bring him to the growing West Texas town, where he's quick to realize its prospects for growth, not only as prime cattle country but also as a transportation hub for westbound settlers and freight wagons—and, in the future, for a railroad line to whose construction the terrain is ideally suited.

Unlike many of the outsiders descending on the town, he's a builder not a ravager, but he must confront the suspicion and hostility of native Texans who fought on the opposite side of the war and now suffer the injustice of the Davis regime and federal occupation troops who keep the administration in power.

Sam's no troublemaker but he's righteous, and when he encounters circumstances that offend his sense of fitness he steps in to set things right. Once the scrapping starts, he's a cyclone of destruction that embodies his last name: Heller.

To Hangtree, too, comes Johnny Cross, long, lean, wolfish—a deadly gunfighter who originally hails from the Texas Panhandle. Now barely out of his teens, he's spent the last few years of the war as a pistol-fighter in Bloody Bill Anderson's mounted band of guerilla irregulars, as part of Quantrill's raiders alongside the likes of Cole Younger and the James brothers. Cross went with fellow Texan Anderson when the latter split from Quantrill to form his own faction. The band fled from the Missouri-Kansas war zone into Texas, where Cross turned against the guerrillas when they began preying on loyal Confederates with the same savagery they'd wielded against the Yankees. When he quit the group and returned to his hometown, his onetime comrades tracked him down and massacred the inhabitants, man, woman, and child, including all his kinfolk.

Cross was gunned down and left for dead but survived. It's hard times in ravaged postwar Texas, but there's always a good living to be made out of killing for a gunman as fast, accurate, and fearless as Johnny Cross. He's a gun for hire—that's business. But no business can hold him when he crosses the trail of any of the men who destroyed his family—that's personal. Texas is vast but time is long and Cross is relentless. There's no opposition too strong or odds too long to thwart him in his vengeance quest.

Sam Heller stands for progress and civilization and will enforce the law with a badge and a gun. Johnny Cross believes only in the law he can make with his pistols. Polar opposites with every reason to hate each other, they form an unlikely friendship to stand beside each other through the years against the evil forces that would destroy the lusty, brawling, fractious folk of Hangtree County.

Until the inevitable day when Heller and Cross must face each other in the final, fatal showdown.

CHAPTER ONE

The preacher named Fulton had presented more sermons than he could count, and long ago lost any fear of speaking before crowds. Second nature for years now. Words flowed from him with the comfortable ease of an autumn breeze through an open window. Strong words, powerful. He'd seen grown men wipe tears under the influence of his sermons, and a time or two, when the Texas summer was at its peak and his oratory brimstone its hottest, watched weaker parishioners faint and drop right off their pews onto the well-worn floor of the Hangtree Church, overwhelmed. When that had happened he'd kept right on preaching while others tended to the overcome ones. Nothing deterred Fulton when he was going full-steam at what he was called to do.

So what, he wondered, was wrong today? Why was he stammering and stuttering so uncharacteristically through his sermon, mind adrift, thoughts roaming off in unwanted directions?

This never happened. He wondered if perhaps he were about to suffer an apoplectic attack of the sort that had killed his grandfather many years before, dropping him like a chopped weed. That grim rumination made it even harder to focus his thoughts.

Embarrassed by his poor performance, Fulton had kept his head lowered through much of the sermon so far, looking at the pages of his open pulpit Bible rather than the faces of his congregation. When he did glance up at them, they looked puzzled. Fulton was glad his wife was home nursing a cold this Sunday; her presence would have heightened his embarrassment.

Fulton actually knew exactly what was wrong with him. The source of his distraction was seated near the rear of the little sanctuary, clad in a dainty gingham dress that brought out the rich blue of her large eyes and enhanced the chestnut color of her thick, piled-up hair. From the moment the young, innocent-looking female stranger had slipped quietly into the church, her mere presence had overcome him. She was a beauty surpassing all others Pastor Fulton had seen in this dusty Texas backwater on the cusp of the Llano Estacado tableland. As a man devoted to righteousness, he habitually made a habit of eschewing anything that might provoke improper thoughts . . . but this young woman, a newcomer to Hangtree, was not making it easy for him. How could he avoid looking at someone seated in his congregation, directly in his line of sight? Each time his eyes swept across her, his thoughts fired off in directions he did not choose. He suspected he was not the only man fighting this particular battle: he'd seen the general reaction of the congregation when she had swept into the church-house and seated herself near the back during the congregational singing of "When I Can Read My Title Clear." Old Deacon Walker, leading the singing, had broken into a coughing fit worthy of a man choking in smoke, but his unblinking seventy-year-old eyes followed the lovely visitor all the way to her pew, his thoughts becoming those of a virile and not particularly devout twenty-year-old man.

Fulton paused, having forgotten his place again. He raised his eyes from the Bible and knew it was hopeless, going on this way. He sighed loudly, leaned forward with forearms resting on the sloped top of the pulpit, and smiled wryly at his humble gathering of saints in a town dominated by sinners.

"I see no point in disputing the obvious: I am ill-prepared for today's service, and am doing a poor job of it. You've noticed it too; I can see it in your faces. I can give you no excuse except to say I have had much on my mind these past days, and it has made me distracted and negligent. I'm sorry, friends. You deserve better, and in the future you shall have it." He closed the Bible and smiled again.

"Are you sick, Preacher?" asked one of the elders in the front row of pews.

"No, Brother Ned. No. Just a lot on my mind lately." He paused, then decided that, since he was lying to God's people right here in God's house, he might as well make the lie a good one. "Family concerns, from back home. My oldest uncle, a man like a father to me, near a century of age now, and finally succumbing to the years. I received the letter this week, and since then have wondered if he is even still among the living. I should not have let it keep me from doing my work as well as you have right to expect."

"We'll stop and pray for the old man right now, if you want, Preacher," said the elder.

"I appreciate that, Ned," Fulton replied. "We'll have that prayer before we leave here today." Fulton gave a tight smile and swept his eyes over the small crowd. They came to rest on the pretty young woman. "We have a guest today. That makes me particularly regret my poor execution of God's work. I'm sorry, miss. Accept my apologies."

She smiled, the image of grace and perfect femininity. Fulton felt his throat tighten and coughed to clear it.

The elder named Ned Randall stood. "Preacher, I feel led to share a verse of scripture that is a favorite of mine. Maybe others here will have verses of their own preference that could stand us in lieu of regular preaching today." Randall straightened his shoulders and spoke his verse. "'I lead in the way of righteousness, in the midst of the paths of judgment, that I may cause those that love me to inherit substance; and I will fill their treasuries.'"

Movement in the right rear corner of the sanctuary pulled Pastor Fulton's eyes away from the beautiful visitor. At first glance it looked like some random heap of old clothing left for the local poor had been dumped on the end of the last pew and was shifting of its own weight, about to fall. A second look revealed the heap to be a man, clad in very tattered clothing and topped with a weathered derby. His garb was too heavy and abundant to be justified by the weather; this was evidently a man of the road who carried his entire wardrobe on his body. Fulton, as distracted all morning, had not previously observed the ragged stranger.

The man stood and lifted his unshaven face. "Hello, Preacher!" he said in a growling, murky voice. "Didn't even know I was here, did you? My greetings to you and the good saints here on this fine Sabbath morning!" He doffed the derby, revealing a shaggy head of graying brown hair, and grinned at the people nearest him, most of whom shifted a few inches farther away. A woman on the far end of his pew rose, crossed the aisle, and took a seat on the other side of the sanctuary.

The ragged man lifted his shaggy chin and said loudly: "Proverbs 8:20 and 21."

Fulton said, "Uh, are you asking me to look those verses up, sir?"

The ragged man shook his head. "No, sir . . .

I'm just 'dentifying that them's the verses quoted by our good brother on the front pew."

"Is he right, Brother Ned?" asked Fulton.

"He's right," said the elder. "Always been favorite verses of mine. I just forgot to cite the reference when I gave them."

Fulton looked back at the tattered fellow. "You know your Bible, sir, seemingly better than I do. May I ask your name?"

"Got a name right out of the Bible, I do. My mama, God rest her, opened her Bible up and stabbed a finger in and told the Lord to guide it to whatever name she was supposed to give me."

"What was it?"

"Well, it wasn't the best one she could have hit. I think she pointed before the Lord had a good enough hold on her finger."

"So . . ." Fulton was beginning to be glad for this strange interruption; it was, at least, more interesting and less humiliating than stammering witlessly through a disjointed sermon while thinking sinful thoughts about a woman half his age . . . a woman come to worship in his own church, no less. He had a lot of repenting to do when he and the Lord found a private moment. "So what is your name?"

The man hung his head. "Judas, sir. Judas Aristocrat."

"I . . . uh, I think you may mean Iscariot."

"That's right! Durn . . . all these years and I always say it wrong. 'Cause that's how my mama said it. She wasn't much for reading, Mama wasn't. Couldn't make out very good on any word with more than four letters."

Fulton looked more closely at the man. "Sir, is that a gunbelt I see?"

"Yes, Preacher. Call me Jude. Folks take to 'Jude' better, y'see."

"Very understandable, Jude. We . . . we ask that guns not be brought into the church-house during worship. It doesn't seem fitting, you know."

"Oh. I'm sorry, sir. I am. Preacher . . . you folks take up an offering on Sundays?"

"We do. Why do you ask?"

"I want to give something."

"Thank you, sir. We'll do that right now. Ushers?"

Four men rose and moved forward to the altar table in front of the pulpit, and there picked up four heavy wooden, deep-sided plates. They divided to the various sides of the two blocks of pews and began passing the plates. Most of the offerings placed in them were meager, though a couple of successful ranchers and a local banker gave more generously.

"I have a question, Preacher," Jude said.

"Very well."

"You told that pretty lady over there you were sorry the service wasn't going good with her being a visitor. Well, me, I'm a visitor too, and you ain't said no such a thing to me."

"I failed to notice you before, sir. I am sorry."

The collection plate reached Jude. "Just a moment," he said, and reached into a pocket.

Producing a few pennies, he dropped them in the plate. The usher moved to pull the plate back, but Jude grabbed his wrist. "Wait. Changed my mind." He reached into the plate and scooped up what he'd dropped in, along with all the other money.

"What the . . . you can't do that!" the usher bellowed. "Once it's in the plate that money belongs to the church."

Jude sighed, rolled his eyes, and drew out the pistol he'd brought into the church-house. Clicking the hammer back, he pointed it at the usher's chest. "I'll have what's in all them plates, friend, and no more lip about it. And the rest of you, start cleaning out your pockets. I'll take coin, bank notes, jewelry, even good folding knives and watches, if you got such."

It took several moments for the congregation as a whole, and Preacher Fulton, to take in what was going on. They were being *robbed*. Robbed in church. Fulton, who had ceased to keep a loaded pistol hidden in the pulpit once the church elders had come up with the no-guns-in-church rule, felt helpless, along with the rest of his congregation.

Except one. One of the offering plates had just reached the beautiful chestnut-haired visitor. With it clutched in her hands, she watched the drama being played out on the other side of the aisle. For once she was not the center of attention, so nobody noticed the peculiar intensity with which she stared at the tattered man with the gun. Quietly she moved out of her pew and across the back of the church toward Jude, who was eyeing the door, planning his flight. He found himself face-to-face with the lady.

"Good God a'mighty!" Judas said. "*You!*"

"Preacher," she shouted toward the front of the church, "I have a verse to share, too! Book of First Pepperday, third chapter, fifth verse: 'And lo, he who desecrated the house of the Lord verily beshat his own teeth on the following morn!'" Then, with a sudden full swing, she pounded the rim of the heavy wooden collection plate very hard against the mouth of the thief, knocking out teeth and ragged pieces of gum, and driving most of the pink-and-crimson mess back into his throat. Jude reflexively swallowed teeth, flesh, and blood as he collapsed to the floor. His pistol fell from a hand gone as limp as the rest of him. Some of the men of the church, once past the shock of the sudden violence from so unexpected a source as a lovely young woman, surrounded the fallen man and commandeered his dropped pistol.

Behind his podium, Preacher Fulton lifted his hands and said, "Brethren, I've seen much in my days as a sinner, and even more in my days as a follower of the Lord, but I have never, *never* seen the like of that! We stand dismissed. And for God's sake, somebody go fetch the law and let's get this scoundrel out of here. Oh, a doctor, too . . . or dentist. Whichever you can find first. Amen and God bless us all."

The pretty woman who had demolished one worship service and one human mouth stood over the crumpled outlaw, from whom blood flowed like a river. "Oh my," she said. "Look what a mess I've made! Oh my!"

CHAPTER TWO

Johnny Cross had chanced to be across the street from the stagecoach stop the day Julia Pepperday Canton had arrived in Hangtree. That had been four days before she and her offering plate punished the intruder at the church service. Cross had been one of about a dozen men lucky enough to witness her emergence from the coach. The vision of an angel placing a delicate foot into a town that had far more in common with hell than heaven had literally stopped him in his tracks and taken his mind off the raw, burning whiskey he'd been on his way to imbibe down at the Dog Star Saloon at that time. The moment he'd seen her he'd removed his hat and tucked his long dark hair more neatly behind his ears, a habit when he spotted lovely women. He wanted to look his best in case she glanced his way. She did, just as he replaced his hat and noticed he'd planted his left boot in a steaming heap left by a passing horse. So much for appearing dignified and dashing before the prettiest visitor ever to grace Hangtree, Texas.

Cross had watched her make her way from the stage stop to the hotel, her luggage carried by a couple of youths she'd recruited with a few bats of her perfectly lashed eyes. Johnny vowed to himself that he'd find his chance to get to know this young woman. He'd make sure it happened.

As it turned out, the chance to meet Julia Canton found him with no effort on his part.

She sat before him now in the small back room at the Hangtree Church where Preacher Fuller had set up a humble library and study for himself. Church offices for preachers were a rarity in frontier outposts such as Hangtree—the notion of a clergyman keeping an office just like a banker or a mayor seemed overly uppity and citified—but Fulton found it easier to prepare his sermons within the walls of a consecrated building, and the privacy of the room made it good for talking with those who came for counsel. He'd been glad to let Cross borrow his study to interview Julia Canton in representation of the meager law enforcement personnel, formal and informal, of Hangtree.

"First off, miss, let me assure you that you are in no trouble," Cross said to the doe-eyed beauty. "What you did in the church Sunday morning, as I understand it, was no assault on your part. It was a defensive act. That bastard . . . pardon me . . . that scoundrel was in the midst of robbing the church and its congregation. Blatant crime. And he was armed and a danger to everyone around him, especially since the elders there decided not to allow guns into the church-house anymore. You were the only person there to have the presence of mind to use something right at hand to stop what the son of a bi . . . uh, gun was doing. I commend you for it."

"Thank you, sir," she said. Her voice made Johnny think of fresh cream. "Where is the man now?"

"Once the doc got his bleeding stopped and stitched up his gums, they locked him up. Yesterday the sheriff hauled him off to the custody of the U.S. Marshal. Winds up he was lying about who he is, all that Judas nonsense. He's a man named Josiah Enoch, known criminal wanted in just about every place a man can be wanted. All kinds of crimes, ranging from murder through bank robbery, highwayman crimes, attempted murder . . . and some I couldn't decently talk about to a lady."

She closed her eyes and gave a little shudder. "To think I was so close to such a bad man!"

"Not the sort you're used to, huh?"

"Oh no. I grew up around good people, and in a good family."

"That's a blessing not to be took for granted, miss."

"Please, call me Julia."

"Call me Johnny." With a fat stub of pencil pulled from a vest pocket, he scrawled her name down on a small paper tablet. She watched him closely. "Why are you taking down notes, Johnny? You said I am not in trouble."

"I'm just trying to go by the book, Julia. Good records make for good law. Got a middle name?"

"Pepperday. My mother's maiden name. She and Papa used to call me Pepper when I was small. I grew up some and decided I liked my first name better. I've gone by Julia ever since."

"Where'd you grow up, Julia?"

"Georgia. Southern to the core. My papa taught me to follow his ways and be true to the South. I have been, all along."

"I carried arms for the South back in the late conflict." He skipped over telling her that the arms he'd carried had been in company with extra-military rebel insurgents, not gray-clad official soldiers. "Which sometimes ain't as 'late' as folks like to imagine it is. Was your father a fighting man?"

"No. A chaplain. Father was an ordained minister before the war, a chaplain throughout, and then a church minister again afterward. He died two years ago. Bad heart."

"I'm sorry. What was his name?"

"George."

Cross faithfully scrawled "George Canton, reverend" on his tablet, though he couldn't have given a sensible reason why. The truth was, he had no good grounds for this interrogation at all. The incident at the church had merely provided a half-believable pretext for spending some time with this pretty young lady, and finding out more about her. He suspected that Julia knew what he was up to. No lady of such loveliness could go through even such a young life as hers without becoming aware of the effect she had on men.

He managed to look serious as he asked her, "Did your late father ever preach from the Book of Pepperday?"

Her eyes twinkled and she grinned. "Heard about me saying that, did you?"

"I was told it by two or three of the folks there in the congregation. They thought it was right funny."

"By the way, it's not just 'Pepperday.' It's 'First Pepperday.'"

"I ain't no Sunday school superintendent, but I don't recall ever seeing a Bible with such a book in it."

She laughed. It sounded like harpsichord music to Johnny Cross. "You'd be hard-pressed indeed to find a copy in any Bible," she said. "I don't know what possessed me to make such a silly joke at a time like that. I just opened my mouth and out it came."

"I heard about the rest of it, too. The part about the wicked man and his teeth, or whatever it was."

She found reason to stare at the top of Preacher Fulton's desk. She was seated in front of the desk, Johnny Cross behind it, in Fulton's chair.

"Oh, dear Lord . . . I'm so ashamed to have been so, so crude!" she said, reddening. "I should never have spoken so in the house of God. It was wrong of me."

Cross shook his head, stifling his smile. "You weren't wrong. He did exactly what you said he would."

"What do you mean?"

"The man you hit with the collection plate. The jailer told me that when he dumped out the overnight slop jars Monday morning, there were that fellow's teeth glittering amidst his mess. He'd 'beshat' his teeth just like you said he would."

She was red-faced, but couldn't help but chuckle. Johnny Cross grinned broadly at her and said, "And don't you worry about being 'crude,' Julia. Crude don't bother me a bit."

She fired him a chiding look, an obvious put-on. He winked at her and she had to grin.

"I guess that man will be wearing waterloos to chew his supper from now on," she said.

"I reckon."

"Why do they call them that, anyway? Waterloos, I mean. What does that have to do with artificial teeth?"

"Well, Julia, you've chanced to ask me something I know the answer to. From what I hear, after that Napoleon fellow fought that big fight at Waterloo, there were so many dead men lying about that some enterprising folks pulled teeth from the corpses, and they were turned into false choppers by them who know how to do such things."

"Oh! What a dreadful thing!"

"That's the way life is, Julia. Dreadful . . . and dreadful hard. Especially in a town like Hangtree, out here on the rump-end of nowhere. This is a rough place. There's some good folk, but plenty of bad ones, too. A lot of both kinds coming and going. Them most prone to linger often seem to run to the bad more than the good."

"I . . . I don't know what reply there is to make to that, Johnny."

"No reply needed. Some things are just what they are. Like Hangtree."

"Why is this place named Hangtree?"

"For an oak here in town where some hangings of bad men were done. It got to be called the 'hangtree,' and the town and county wound up with the same name."

"I see."

"Tree's still standing. You'll see it, if you ain't already."

She picked at a cuticle. "A harsh town, it seems."

"Yep. Which leads me to a question I'm obliged to ask you."

"Yes?"

"What would draw a fine young woman with good breeding and religious family roots to come to such a place as this? Alone?"

"Are . . . are you sure I'm in no trouble? If what I did was justified . . ."

"You're not in trouble, Julia. I'm asking that question for personal reasons. You interest me. And seeing someone as, well, *unexpected* as you in a place like this . . . it's hard to figure out."

She sighed and looked sad. "I don't mind telling you, because you seem quite nice. I came here exactly because it is, as you put it, the 'rump-end of nowhere.' It wasn't so much a manner of running to something, or someplace, as it was running away. I came here because of . . . an affair of the heart. One that went badly. One that hurt me. Left me alone. And where I was back in Georgia, among people who knew my family so well, I felt every eye in town on me at every moment. Being judged, talked about, stared at . . . you understand."

"Seems to me that long ago you'd have been used to being talked about and stared at. You're a very pretty young woman, Julia. You're bound to know that. You've probably been stared at all your life."

"I . . . I . . . yes."

"But why Hangtree, of all places? There's a lot of nowhere places a gal from Georgia could hide without ranging out this far."

"That's true . . . but if I'd gone to any of those other places, wouldn't the same question still apply? Why there and not somewhere else? I wanted to get away from Georgia, off in a place nobody has heard of and would never figure me to go. Here I am."

"Here you are. I've got to admit to you, I'm glad of it. And I've never been one to beat around the bush. I'd like to ask you if I might call on you some, since you're here with us. And unattached."

She stared back at him.

"Am I talking too forthright, Julia?"

"No . . . not really. It's just that for me, right now, it's just too soon. My heart is still broken and God only knows how long it will be until it has healed."

"I understand."

"Even so, I'm honored by your interest."

"All I'm asking is to spend a little time with you. Maybe to make this town a little easier to abide for a young woman alone and away from home. I just want to be friendly."

She smiled. "Thank you. I have nothing against friendliness, so my answer is yes. Now, might you recommend for me a boardinghouse? I am living in a hotel room and would like to find something better for a longer term, with meals provided."

"Shall we take a walk? I can show you just such a place."

"Yes, thank you. Are you finished with me here, then?"

"For now . . . but let me ask you once more: Are you certain you had never met the man in the church before? And that he could not know you?"

"I did not know him. Whether he has seen me before, how can I know?"

Cross drew in a deep breath. "Air's a little close in here. Let's take a walk."

Chapter Three

The sound of a fast-sweeping broom and a whistled barn dance tune told Johnny Cross who he and Julia would encounter as they rounded the alleyway corner beside Lockhart's Emporium, the biggest general store in the region. Sure enough, Timothy Holt was there on the front boardwalk, sweeping and whistling mightily. When the simple-minded young man of twenty-two saw Johnny Cross, his face lit with a smile broader than the brim of his flop hat. When he noticed Julia Canton, the smile became a nervous grimace.

Cross had seen Hangtree's resident simpleton lose his nerve in the presence of the town's plainest girls. Such a one as the flawless Julia Canton was almost too much for him.

"Hi . . . hi, Johnny." Timothy's eyes shifted to Julia and back again, very fast.

"Howdy, Tim. See you're hard at it again today."

"Gotta work hard, Johnny. Gotta work hard for Mr. Lockhart."

"He is still paying you enough to make it worth your while, ain't he?"

"He pays me every week on Friday, Johnny. Sometimes he gives me a bonus if I do extra good. You know what a bonus is, Johnny?"

"I do. Wish somebody would throw a few my way from time to time."

"And he lets me and my mama buy things here at a dis . . . dis . . ."

"A discount?"

"That's right! I forget that word sometimes. A discount." He mouthed it silently to himself two or three more times.

Julia took a step toward Timothy, small hand extended. "Mr. Holt, was it?"

Timothy stared down at her hand like he was afraid of it. "I'm . . . just Timothy, ma'am. Just plain Timothy. Ain't never been a mister."

"Won't you shake my hand, Timothy? I'm very pleased to meet you. My name is Julia Canton."

He gaped at the hand like it was charged with lightning. His eyes flicked up to her face and she smiled at him. Timothy nervously edged his own hand forward, sucked in a breath, and grabbed her hand with his eyes closed. He shook her hand with such vigor her entire arm danced.

"Pleased to meet you, ma'am. I'm Timothy." He paused, frowning. "But I already told you that . . . oh, dang, I'm so stupid sometimes!"

He squeezed her hand too hard, distracted by anger at himself.

Johnny Cross touched Timothy's shoulder. Timothy opened his eyes. "You don't need to crush her hand plumb off, Tim. She might need it again one of these days."

Timothy froze and stared at Julia's face with eyes gone wide. "I'm . . . I'm sorry, ma'am," he said. "I didn't mean to be squeezing your hand so hard. I was just . . . just pleased to get to meet you, that's all. I like nice people. That's why I like Johnny. He's nice to me."

Julia put on a playful frown and flicked her eyes at Johnny Cross. "But not to other people? Is that what you mean, Timothy?"

"Oh, no, no, ma'am! He's nice to a lot of people. Bad folks, though, mean folks, he ain't nice to them."

"Well, that's how it should be, I suppose," Julia said. "Timothy, it's such a pleasure to meet you! You've done a good job of sweeping here . . . I've never seen so clean a boardwalk!"

"I try hard, ma'am. If I don't, Mr. Lockhart, he'll say to me, 'Tim boy, there's as much dirt on the boardwalk as there is in the street.'" Timothy paused and laughed at the feeble humor while Johnny Cross threw in a forced-but-believable laugh of his own. Julia caught on and laughed as well for Timothy's benefit.

Timothy beamed at her. "You're nice, ma'am. I can tell you are. And pretty, too."

"That she is, Tim," Cross said.

"Mr. Lockhart, he has a daughter name of Faye. She's pretty." Timothy said. He sidled just a little closer and added, "But you're prettier. Ain't she, Johnny?"

"Let me give you some advice, Timothy: You're best off not comparing women to each other, not out loud, anyway. It'll come back to bite you every time."

"Oh. Sorry then. But you are pretty. And I think you're nice."

Julia beamed him a smile. "You know what, Timothy? I think you are nice, too. I'll bet you are one of the nicest young men in Hangtree! Would you say he was, Johnny?"

"He's a fine gent all around, sure 'nough, Julia. Timothy speaks the truth as he sees it, but he generally speaks only that part of it that helps folks and makes them grin."

"A good policy," Julia said.

Timothy seemed more serious all at once and looked down at his feet. "Ma'am, I don't know if you can tell it or not, but I'm . . . I'm not . . . not smart."

"There's different kinds of smart," Julia said. "Or so has been my experience in knowing men. Most aren't as smart as they think they are."

"I bet you know a lot of men," Timothy said. "I mean . . . you being pretty and all, I bet a lot of men want to know you."

"In the full-out biblical sense," Cross muttered beneath his breath, a thought spoken out loud that should have been kept silent, because Julia heard it, and understood it though Timothy didn't. Johnny grimaced and played out a mental vision of himself kicking his own backside.

"Are you going to live in Hangtree, Miss Julia?" Timothy asked.

"For a time, at least," she said. "Maybe for a long time . . . it depends on whether I find reason to stay. And if I like the people, and the town, and so on. What about you, Timothy? Do you like the people, and the town?"

"Most the time," he said, shrugging. "A lot of them are nice folks. Sometimes some of them are kind of mean. They pick on me and make fun."

"Oh, I'm so sorry!" Julia said. "It's so wrong when people do that. So wrong!"

"One time I was sweeping and this man got behind me and started acting like he was sweeping, too, and making a face that made him look stupid. My mama always tells me to just act like people like that ain't there and they'll go away. But this man didn't. Not until Johnny came along and knocked him off the walk into the street. Then he got his arm around the man's neck and hauled him back up in front of me and made him tell me he was sorry."

"Did he?"

"Yes. Then he left Hangtree because he was scared of Johnny after that."

Julia smiled beautifully.

"Timothy, I do like you," she said. "You remind me of someone I knew for a long time, and loved very much. However long I'm in Hangtree, I'd like to be your friend."

Timothy smiled and nodded. When Julia moved in and gave him a gentle hug around the shoulders, his face reddened and he backed away without another word, and went back to sweeping. He did not take his eyes off Julia until she and Johnny had walked around a corner and out of sight.

"Did you really know somebody like Timothy?" Cross asked her. "Or were you just talking?"

"I knew somebody. His name was Jimmy. He was simple in his mind. Like a little boy. Like Timothy seems to be. He was my brother."

"Was?"

"He died. His heart was weak from the time he was a baby."

"I'm sorry. Younger brother?"

"Yes. The last of us."

"How many brothers and sisters in your family?"

"My older brother, Lloyd. One older sister, Betty. Then me. Then poor Jimmy." Julia sniffed and dabbed at an eye.

"The others still living?"

"Lloyd died in a skirmish in Georgia, coming home when the war was over. Betty married a Yankee and lives in Maine now. We haven't spoken in years. Marrying a Yankee! A shame to the family."

"I got little stomach for that breed myself," Cross said. "Took shots at enough of them, and them back at me."

"I'm hopeful I'll not run into many Yankees here in Texas," she said.

"There are a few. Carpetbaggers come down to tell us how to live our lives and take whatever they can from us, mostly. And a few folks who lived here when it all started and just didn't see things the right way and favored the bluebellies. Hard to account for, but there were some like that."

"I deplore that kind. There were even some in Georgia."

Johnny said, "There's a carpetbagger in Hangtown that puts a twist in my guts like nobody else. Name of Sam Heller."

She'd been looking across the street, but snapped her head around at the mention of the name.

"You know him?" Cross asked her.

"How would I know anybody in this godforsaken town?"

"You just reacted when I said his name, that's all."

"Well, maybe I heard somebody mention him on the stagecoach while they were looking at the cattle herds out on the plains. Who is he?"

"He's a crack shot and a stout fellow. And brave. I'll give him that. The kind of man you want on your side in a fight."

"But he's not your friend, being a Yankee?"

"We've got our own way of getting on with each other. We get by. Every now and then get to hating each other for a few days. It don't last."

"What's he do?"

"Cattleman. Richest man to be found hereabouts for miles around."

"How rich?"

"A lot of them cattle you folks in the stage were looking at, they were Heller's. He's got maybe a thousand head of longhorns with his brand on them. And story has it he's got a hundred thousand dollars or more in cash and gold in the Hangtree Bank. But you know how stories like that go. He may have that much, may have less. Hell, he may have a lot more. Wouldn't surprise me."

"I'll have to meet him."

"Nah. You've met me, and that should be good enough for you. But once Heller sees you he'll make sure you meet him. And you'll know him. Generally wears that yaller hair of his long and tucked back behind his ears."

"Sort of like you do, minus the yellow part."

"Well . . . I guess so. He dresses to catch the eye. Bandoliers crossing his chest and a sawed-off Winchester Model 1866 rifle in place of a pistol. And he can hit what he wants with that mule's-leg, let me tell you."

"'Mule's-leg?'"

"That's what folks out here call a sawed-off rifle."

"I've got a lot to learn about Texas."

"Well, let me tell you something you're going to learn soon enough: You earned yourself an admirer already."

"Why . . . Johnny! I'm flattered! Are you always so forthright about your feelings?"

"Well . . . yeah, I am, but this time it ain't me I'm talking about. I'm talking about poor old Timothy back there at the Emporium. I know that boy well. Good boy, going to be a child all his days. Innocent as a lamb. But he's got a man's feeling for the ladies, and a heart that attaches fast to any pretty thing who wanders by and gives him the time of day. Right now that pretty thing is you."

"Oh, I suppose he might get an infatuation, Johnny, but I'm accustomed to that."

"I bet you are. And Timothy won't be the only one who'll get his heart set on you. You'll have the eye of every gent in town, not just the dummies, before you're here another week."

"Are you going to be among them, Johnny?"

"Already am, Julia. Already am."

"Let's walk some more, Johnny. You need to show me that boardinghouse. Oh, and please don't call Timothy a 'dummy.' Some used to call my brother that. I always hated it."

"I'm sorry, then. Let's go."

"Walk me past the bank. I want to see the bank."

"The bank ain't much to look at."

"I need to know where it is. I didn't come to Hangtree without some degree of means. I'll be needing to open myself a bank account here."

"Beauty, a good brain, common sense. And grit. And apparently a bit of money, too."

"A bit. I'd like to make it a lot more."

Johnny Cross chuckled. "You're the full combination, lady. It really ain't going to be only poor old Timothy trailing around after you."

"I'm counting on that, Johnny Cross. I came here to move my life ahead, not backward."

"Meaning?"

"Wait and see. Just wait and see."

"Miss Julia Canton, I'm beginning to think you came to Hangtree in hopes of finding yourself a good Texas man to marry. Which makes this a fine time indeed to be a Texas man. And I reckon I'm the luckiest of them all, being the first to trot you around town like this, right in front of God and everybody."

"I guess you are, Johnny Cross. Now step it up! I like to walk fast."

"Me, I kind of want to stretch this one out."

She grasped his arm and tugged at him. "Come on, pokey. Lively now!"

"Pretty. But bossy."

"Don't you forget it, Mr. Cross."

CHAPTER FOUR

The vehicle moving along the Hangtree Trail was nondescript, a mere plain-sided box enclosing the tail end of a wagon. Equally unremarkable was the man driving it.

He would have looked at home behind a bookkeeper's desk, ringing a schoolmaster's bell in the doorway of a small-town school, or shelving books in a library. Thin, short-statured, he carried on bony shoulders a balding head a little too large for his thin stalk of a neck. He held the leads with hands made to accommodate stubby fingers, but bearing instead long and supple ones. No odder human creature, Mexican, Comanche, or Anglo, had ever traveled through this flat and barren-looking landscape than had Otto Perkins, traveling photographer.

He'd learned his craft in the hardest school of all: the battlefields of the American South. Blessed with the patronage of a wealthy uncle who was fascinated by the science of photography and freely spent his fortune supporting the development of increasingly better photographic equipment, the Atlanta native Otto had joined his uncle and a local embalmer in a morbid but educational wartime enterprise. They toured bloodied, smoking battlefields and photographically recorded the carnage with unflinching candor, like Confederate Mathew Bradys. They also created much more sanitized and dignified images of the dead whose bodies remained sufficiently intact to allow cleaning and embalming. These they dressed and photographed on portable, collapsible draped biers they carried with them on a wagon. Images of their dead in poses that made them appear merely to be peacefully sleeping, cleansed of blood and grit and with wounds hidden, were welcomed by bereaved families, most of whom were willing to scrape together whatever they could to purchase those final mementos of the lost ones.

Thus, throughout the war, bespectacled Otto Perkins learned to be perhaps the finest unheralded photographer to come out of the southland. He discovered as well a gift for business, a tolerance for blood and mayhem, and a mounting fascination with death, especially that inflicted by violence. And so, when the war had ended, Otto had created his mobile, wagon-mounted darkroom, and headed west in hopes of building a fortune at best, making a living at least.

In his many long hours of traveling alone, bouncing along on his darkroom wagon and wincing at the potential of every jolt to loosen some seam or joint and create a light leak in his mobile darkroom, Otto had been forced to admit to himself that it all was easier than he'd imagined it would be. With no plan worthy of the name, he'd traveled from town to town, state to territory and back again, and along the way found plenty of people eager to have images of their lives in a growing country turned into something they could hold in their hands and treasure for their entire lives. Otto photographed newborn babies, barn-raisings, cattle brandings, weddings, funerals (complete with corpses laid out or propped up in their finest clothing with family circled around), and even a few hangings, legal and otherwise. What he'd found himself most interested in, however, were photographs related to criminal violence and the criminals who made that happen. It had become something of a secret specialty of his, taking photographs of the infamous and dangerous. He'd photographed the James brothers and their cohorts, and others who had made their names known in the violence of Bleeding Kansas and the border wars, including Quantrill and Bloody Bill Anderson. He'd taken a photograph of the latter with some of his best pistol fighters, including one young and fine-looking dark-haired fellow whose name Otto could not for the life of him remember, but whose image had for Otto become the single best visual embodiment of the pistol fighters of Missouri-Kansas.

Otto Perkins had plans. He would be the creator of the finest library of photographs of the late war and the rebuilding and growth of the nation in the years following. Particularly the expansion into the West. And he would chronicle as his specialty the world of outlawry that was inevitably part of any expanding frontier. As he traveled the West seeking any way he could find for his camera to make him a dollar, he would in particular capture the images of the bad men and their victims, and someday it all would make him famous and envied, respected, rich, and remembered. Otto could feel it in his rather frail bones.

And so, over time his life quest had attained an increasingly narrow focus, his routes and travels guided by rumors and hints and chatter he picked up along the way. He went where he believed he could find those who did not wish to be found, the ones who kept themselves in the places where civilization and law had yet to fully take root.

He had to find them, after all, before he could have any hope of photographing them.

It was his quest that drove him now toward the grubby Texas backwater of Hangtree. Following a trail of rumors and talk, in search of a particular human being.

Otto's awareness that he was not alone on this road came to him gradually, and when a look back around the side of his wagon confirmed the presence of a rider coming along behind, it merely verified something Otto had already sensed in some manner unknown even to himself. So there was no surprise involved.

Except in regard to the appearance of the lone rider. The man gave the immediate impression of some ancient Norse warrior thrust forward in time. He was tall and broad-shouldered, muscled torso narrowing to a lean waist. His hair was flowing and mane-like, golden yellow, framing a weathered blue-eyed face both rugged and handsome. The kind of man who had intimidated Otto Perkins all his days.

But also a man who visually embodied the rugged masculinity of the westerner to a degree seldom encountered. Otto had pointed his camera at enough lawmen and outlaws and brawlers and toughs to know that most did not even vaguely match the vision of America's public of the quintessential man of the frontier. Yellow, broken teeth, skin weathered and sunned to the texture of over-abused leather, warts and scars and cauliflowered noses and squinted eyes, fingers resembling ill-bent twigs from long-past untended breaks . . . Otto had photographed hundreds of such, many of them outlaws and desperadoes.

This man, though, this silent and unexpected fellow man of the road brought by fate to this point of meeting . . . such visually classic subjects as this one almost never came along.

It was time to seize the moment. Otto pulled

his wagon over to the side of the Hangtree Road and reined it to a halt. As expected, the gold-maned rider—who wore a sawed-down Winchester rifle holstered on his right thigh, rode over and halted beside the wagon.

"Howdy," said Otto, peering at the man through the thick lenses of his spectacles.

"Howdy yourself," said the other. "Having trouble with your wagon?"

"No, sir, not at all. I've just stopped to get some grub out for a bite of lunch. Name's Otto Perkins. Have you had aught to eat, stranger?"

The horseman moved closer and thrust a leathery hand toward the wagoneer. They shook, Otto noticing the strength of the rider's grip. "I'm Heller, Sam Heller, Mr. Perkins. Herd a few cattle and such as that around these parts."

"Call me Otto, sir."

"Call me Sam. What's your game, friend? I believe you're a newcomer."

"I am. If you've got a couple of minutes to spare I'll put some meat on some bread and pour us some cider, and we can eat a bit and I'll show you what I do."

"I hate to deprive a man of victuals he might need for himself at a later time," said Heller. "But my growling belly would make me out a liar if I claimed lack of hunger. I thank you for the invite and will be glad to join you."

"Excellent, Sam. Excellent."

* * *

The sandwiches were dry and the meat tough, but the Arkansas cider mostly remedied both. They ate and drank and perused some of the photographs Otto Perkins carried with him as a sort of professional calling card. Heller was impressed and said so, and with the skill of a Union man accustomed to surviving in old rebel country, managed to avoid a discussion of their relative positions during the late war, images of which were mixed in among the photos Perkins showed. Heller could tell from the prevalence of Union corpses in the photographs, and from Otto's drawl, that he was dealing with a Confederate-leaning man here. But also a man of great talent in his field. Heller was not one to gush out compliments to any man, but the praise he gave to Otto's work was sincere.

"So what brings you out to the devil's armpit, Otto Perkins?" Heller asked.

"Devil's armpit . . . by which you mean . . ."

"Hangtown. Hangtree. The town up the road."

Otto chuckled politely. "Well, sir, what brings me here is the same thing that takes me anywhere I go: my work. I come to this empty wilderness in search of images that can intrigue and reveal and teach. Images of the people who have gravel and grit in their souls so they not only survive in this difficult land, but even thrive."

"You sound like a professor, friend Perkins. Not that I've known many such in my day."

"Which? Professors, or people fit to survive out here?"

"Either."

"Well, Sam, if I sound to you like a professor, then you, sir, sound like, and look like . . . this." Otto waved his hand to indicate the land around them.

"Like that, huh?" Heller looked around at the endless brush-studded flatness around them. "I fail to see the resemblance, myself."

"I mean you look like the spirit of it all. A human incarnation of what makes this country so tough and stern and strong. That's why, Sam Heller, I hope you'll let me create a portrait of you once we reach Hangtown. Perhaps you standing before the famous hangtree itself."

"I . . . I ain't much one for having my picture took."

"It requires nothing of you. Simplicity personified. You take your position, remain for the brief time it takes to capture the image, and that's it."

"I'll consider it, Otto. Because you seem a decent enough hombre. Better than many I've run across on this same road."

Otto's heart skipped a beat. "Outlaws, you mean? Bad men?"

Heller nodded, one fast bob of the head. "Hangtree draws its share, and I've dealt with many."

Otto all but rubbed his hands together in glee. "Excellent!"

"How so?"

"I have my own reasons, artistic and commercial, for expressing that feeling. You see, it is my goal to gather the finest and most complete photographic gallery of those individuals and groups who have brought romance and mythos and a sense of legend to the world of the western outlaw . . . those whose names will be recalled through the years. I hope to allow their faces to be remembered as well. Too many will come and go and all that will remain will be legends and lies and faulty memories. As a photographer I can remedy that."

"So you're going to Hangtree in the hope of lining up robbers and killers and rapers and may-hemers and saying 'smile!'"

"Not precisely how I'd phrase it, but essentially, yes."

"We all live in our own worlds, don't we, Otto."

"We do. But in my view, we should learn to remember as much as we can of all of them. We need help for that. Giving some of that help is what I do."

Heller finished his sandwich, dusted off his hands, and said, "Well sir, I wish you luck in whatever thing it is you're working at. I don't profess to understand arty things real well. But I got to tell you that I hope you're disappointed. I hope there's not an outlaw to be found in Hangtree when we get there. They're just too much dang trouble for honest folks."

CHAPTER FIVE

Though the general flatness of the country-
side disguised it, there was a gentle swell to the
land between the place they were and the nearest side of Hangtree. Thus they had no idea, until
they had moved forward a few hundred yards,
that a dead man was lying beside the road.
He'd not been there long enough to be much
decayed, but the buzzards had already relieved
him of his eyes and lines of ants were moving
into his ears and out again while others entered
via his nose and slightly open, sun-blistered lips.
Buzzards had also helped themselves to what
brains they could reach through the bullethole
in his forehead, and insects were also swarming
freely around that splintery access point as well.
It was an ugly sight that Sam Heller did not like
looking at, though he'd seen enough gore in his
day to handle it. Otto Perkins, delicate-looking
as he was, seemed to possess no qualms at all

about getting near the stinking body. This photographer of the dead leaned over the ruined face, whose skin crawled with bugs and swarmed with flies, and studied it seriously.

"I've seen this man," he said.

"Who is he?" asked Heller.

"I'm not sure. His features are very damaged, as you can see. And besides that, I'm not sure I could place him. I see so many faces in my line of work."

"Well, Otto, we can bury him, throw him up on top of your wagon there and haul him on into Hangtree, or . . ."

"Not on top of the wagon. He'd leak right through the wood into my darkroom box, and it's close and hot in there. I'd never be able to use it again. I say we leave him where he is. Or drape him over the saddle of your horse and ride him in that way. Or we could drag him with a rope."

"Leave him and report that he's out here," Heller said. "If the critters don't have him scattered off in all directions before you know it, somebody can come out here and say a few words over him and put him in a hole."

Otto Perkins rubbed his chin between thumb and forefinger. "It doesn't seem right to leave him out here when I know I've seen him before."

Heller said, "You don't want him leaking into your wagon box, and I don't want him staining up my saddle. So it looks like it's drag him or leave him. Your choice."

Perkins paced about in a tense circle. "Drag, then. I can't think of leaving him here."

"Drag it is."

"But not until I take a picture."

"I don't think this gent is up to smiling for the camera, Otto."

"I have to have an image. I have to be able to figure out why he seems familiar."

"Suit yourself. But I don't think you'll find many people wanting to put that face in a frame and hang it over the mantelpiece."

"It's for my own purposes, which I've already explained. It won't take long. If you prefer, go on ahead toward town."

"I'll wait. I want to see how you do what you do."

It made for an ugly parade. Heller brought up the front on horseback, Otto Perkins and his dark-room wagon behind him, and the stiffened dead man, tied at the ankles and freshly photographed, dragging along behind like a sculpture made of pulpwood, shedding pieces of decaying flesh along the way and tainting the air all around with the smell of death.

Squint McCray and Luke Pettigrew, the former the proprietor of the scruffy Dog Star Saloon and the latter a frequent friend and companion of Johnny Cross, were among the first to notice their approach. Sam Heller, looking like he always did and being a commonly seen personage in Hangtown, did not particularly attract their eye, but Otto Perkins and his boxy wagon did. Once proximity and angle allowed them to see that a human form was being dragged behind the wagon, their full attention was seized and held, and both men headed out to meet Heller, Squint with his good eye almost as pinched as his permanently squinted one because of dust blowing against his face, and Pettigrew with his pegleg slowing him down this particular day more than it usually did. Some days for the war-crippled ex-Confederate were just that way. At times he could actually feel pain in the ankle of a foot no longer there.

The pair muttered greetings at Heller and nodded cautiously at the pencil-necked man driving the boxed-in wagon, then moved around to the battered corpse. They stood beside it, wincing at the stench and ugliness, and looked for any clue as to why a dead man was being dragged into town by Sam Heller and some puny stranger.

Heller, on foot now with his horse loosely tied off to a front wheel of Otto Perkins's wagon, walked around and stood beside Pettigrew.

"Who is he, Sam?" Squint McCray asked.

"Don't know," Heller replied. "We found him out on the road like this, dead and stinking like the rump of Satan, blowflies buzzing and ants crawling and the buzzards sitting around and belching from having eat a good meal. Mr. Perkins, who I met coming in toward town, he says the man looks familiar to him, but he can't place him."

Pettigrew cast a quick glance at Heller. "Did this Perkins maybe shoot this man?"

"Don't seem likely. This gent had been laying out there long enough to start ripening pretty good, as you can see and smell for yourself. And I had already come upon Mr. Perkins when we found him. I can tell you, just from watching him, that he was as surprised to find this corpse as I was."

"Who is this Perkins?" asked Pettigrew.

"Traveling picture-taking man. Got himself set up so he can work right out of his wagon there . . . that box is made so no light gets in and he can work in there with the pictures he takes. He took one of our dead friend here. That's what he does, mostly. Makes pictures of killed folks and outlaws. Other things, too, but it's the outlaws and killers and such he likes best."

Pettigrew frowned. "Sounds like an odd bird."

"Yep," Heller said.

As if cued by the conversation, Perkins came around from the front of the wagon. With lips pressed nervously together, he nodded briefly at each man and got nods and grunts of greeting in return. Perkins looked down at the corpse.

"He looks even worse since we dragged him," he said. "Does he look familiar to any of you?"

"Sure does," said a voice from behind them.

Sheriff Mack Barton walked up beside Heller and took a look at the dead man. "Yep, I know that face . . . or what's left of it."

"Who is he?" Pettigrew asked.

"Ever heard of the Toleen brothers?"

"Oh, yes!" exclaimed Perkins. "They rode with the Bracken Gang for years, but made their name riding for Black Ear Skinner and his men. Some of the worst. I made portraits of both of them, along with Black Ear himself and some of his other gunnies. That's where I saw this man before."

"Black Ear Skinner . . . God!" said Barton. "Worst of the worst, that one was. I'm glad he's gone."

"Over in Mason, wasn't it?" Pettigrew said. "During a stage robbery?"

"That's right. Shot right through the side of the head. The side that had the blackened ear, matter of fact."

"How'd that happen to him, anyway, sheriff? The ear, I mean."

"As I hear it, it was somebody who had a grudge against Skinner's old man, his pa. To pay him back for whatever he'd done, they captured his boy, Curry—that being Black Ear before he was Black Ear—and hauled him off in the woods somewheres, and made him suffer bad. Cut him, beat him, whipped him. Burned him. Burned off three toes, burned his elbows through to the bone, and burned his left ear to ash. The elbows healed over, but the joints were stiffer than they should have been. The ear never grew back in, not most of it, anyway . . . just left him with a black little stub of gristle sticking off the side of his head. Earned him the nickname Black Ear. He hated being called that when he was young, but by the time he'd growed up and turned to crime, he accepted it. Liked the sound of calling his gang the 'Black Ears.' From all the stories, though, his heart was blacker than that ear ever was. Man had no mercy at all in him. One of his own gang crossed him, just a young gent who wore his hair long, and Black Ear hung him up by his toes and built a fire under his head. Kept it low enough just to cook him, not burn him fast. Burned off that long hair down to the scalp, then burned the scalp through to the skull. He let the poor hombre suffer for half an hour or more, then built the fire up higher and tossed the boy a pistol with one bullet in it. Told him he could use it to shoot him, Black Ear, or put the bullet through his own brain. The boy did what anybody would in that circumstance and used it on himself."

"The hell," said Pettigrew. "Reckon that's true, or just one of them stories that get started and grow?"

"It's true," Perkins said. "I heard it spoken of by Black Ear himself. He laughed about how after the poor devil shot himself, the blood that dropped down sizzled when it hit the fire."

"Meaner than a Comanche with an Apache mama and a bad affliction of piles," Heller muttered.

"Yes indeed."

"And this poor fellow here was one of Black Ear's guns, huh?"

"He was. He and his brother together, twins. Drew and Cal Toleen."

"Which one is this?"

Perkins rubbed his chin in the same way Heller had seen him do out on the Hangtree Trail. "Don't know. They look just alike to everybody except them who knows them well. This one could be either one, as best I could tell. I've only had one good look at the Toleens myself."

"But there's no question it's one of the two?"

"No, sir," said Perkins.

"You weren't talking so sure before. You said he was familiar but you couldn't place him."

"That's right . . . then the sheriff here called his name and then I remembered, and knew he was right."

"So where's his brother?" Luke Pettigrew asked. "Every story I've heard of them, they always stuck together. You see one, you're going to see t'other before you know it."

"Maybe the other one's dead, too," said the sheriff. "If he is, we ought to go have a drink to celebrate. Any of the Black Ears gone is good news to good folk."

"Tell you what, men, this old boy here needs to be in the ground."

"Needed to be in it maybe two days ago," said Heller, waving his hand in front of his nose to clear some of the death stench. "I'd say it's time to get this gent here a new low-ceiling house made of pine boards, if you know what I mean."

"I'll fetch him myself," said Barton.

CHAPTER SIX

Myrtle Bewley already had played a part in the commerce of three small towns in her fifty-year life: she'd worked as a young girl in her uncle's general store in rural Kentucky, stocking shelves and sweeping floors; at a slightly older age she'd been trained as a seamstress by an aunt in Illinois, and found work in a dress shop, hemming new dresses and repairing torn ones. After marrying, she and her husband had opened a general mercantile, also in Illinois, until the war erupted and Bradley Bewley found himself drawn into the life of a soldier. Wartime friendships and interactions had led him to a conviction that his most promising future might lie in the cattle business, which with the growth of railroads and westward expansion of a reunifying nation, seemed poised to move forward when the war was past. So without much delay the childless couple headed to Texas, following a particular army friend, Dan Roark, who guided them into

Hangtree County. Like many others, Roark and Bewley began building their own small ranching operation, developing their herd mostly from the unbranded and free-ranging cattle spread across the plains. And to make his wife happy, Bradley Bewley had supported her wish to create a business of her own in the town of Hangtree. A dress shop, of all things, a small, bright haven of domesticity nestled among saloons, gambling halls, dives, dance parlors, cantinas pandering to Mexican tastes, general merchandise stores, a livery stable, freight depot, a feed and farm supply store, and several brothels. Unlikely as it seemed, even to Myrtle herself, the dress shop had fared well, welcomed by the lonely, isolated wives and daughters of Hangtree and its environs. Never quite thriving, the business even so survived and moved ahead.

Myrtle was on a ladder, dusting a high shelf at the back of the store, when the door opened and a lovely young woman entered. This was a newcomer, never seen before by the shopkeeper. Myrtle welcomed the sight of her because she was well-dressed and seemed a likely spender. Myrtle descended the ladder and approached her.

"Good day, miss . . . I am Myrtle Bewley, proprietress of this shop. Hello and welcome!"

"I am Julia Pepperday Canton. I am so pleased to find that Hangtree has a dress shop."

"Thank you, Miss Canton. I'm happy you like it. I do find it makes this town a little less rough, a little more hospitable to those of our sex. You are new to Hangtree, I believe?"

"I am. And I am here alone, so I welcome your cordiality."

"Alone? I am surprised such a lovely young woman as you are is not married."

"Thank you for the compliment. Marriage is a blessing I hope will come to me in the future. Assuming, of course, I can find the right man."

"Maybe right here in Hangtree, miss!"

"Perhaps so." Julia looked about, making sure there were no other customers in the shop. "Maybe you can, sometime or another, provide me some eligible names."

"Surely. I might mention one even now . . . have you heard the name of Sam Heller?"

"I think I have."

"He is a man of means. Owns more cattle, and has more money in the Hangtree Bank, than any other man in this county and a good distance beyond. Some don't like him because he was a Union man in the late conflict . . . but we must all learn to put such former differences behind us, don't you think? The wise woman keeps her eyes focused on her future rather than on the past. And only the foolish woman disregards the importance of monetary stability."

"You are a fount of good advice, Mrs. Bewley! I shall have to visit you often."

"You will be welcome. I am open daily, though I do close in the afternoon on Wednesdays. And on Sundays, of course."

"Of course."

Julia perused the little store's bolts of cloth and spools of thread and flats of needles, pins, and scissors. Meanwhile Myrtle Bewley chattered on, pleased to have a seemingly moneyed customer willing to listen to her. Julia pleased Myrtle further when she purchased a simple but colorful handmade shawl Myrtle had stitched and decorated herself.

With her purchase draped over her shoulders, Julia headed for the door, but stopped short of opening it. "Oh my," she said.

"What's wrong?" Myrtle asked.

"Nothing . . . not really. It's just . . . someone is out there I don't really prefer to run into."

"Oh! Who might it be?"

Julia sighed loudly. "There's a young man in town, simple in his mind, who has taken a liking to me because I was kind to him. I was warned that he might misinterpret my friendliness as something other than it is, and become infatuated. I'm afraid that might be the case."

"I'm sure it's Timothy from the Emporium who you are speaking of," Myrtle said. "A good boy. Good heart but simple mind."

"Yes, it is Timothy I'm speaking of. I have some affection for him because I had a brother in a similar situation, and loved him very much. But Timothy, I think, sees me in a more romantic light than I would wish. I hate to hurt him, though."

"Is Timothy out there right now, then?"

"Waiting for me on the porch across the street. With a paper flower in his hand."

"How sweet! They sell those for a penny at the Emporium where he sweeps. But I understand your concern. How to be kind without hurting his feelings? It's a difficult question. Perhaps it will help you to know that this isn't the first time poor Tim has become smitten like this. I've seen it before. And he came through it without being damaged."

"Who was the lady?"

"Lady! Ha!" Myrtle shook her head and frowned. "No lady, that one! It's hardly decent to speak of, really. It was one of our local doves. Do you know what I mean by that?"

"A *soiled* dove, I assume."

"Yes. Hard-looking young woman, face like a piece of flint, but Timothy seemed to see something in her he liked. Not in a lewd way, I don't think. He simply sees the good in people that most of us don't."

"Not a bad thing, I suppose," Julia said.

"I'm sure you're right. But this time Timothy's infatuation very nearly got him killed."

"Oh my! How?"

"Timothy lives in a little back-alley house with his widowed mother, but when he isn't working he often simply roams the streets. The chef at the restaurant of the Cattleman Hotel slips him food to take home, which helps him and his mother greatly. Other people are kind to him, too. And a lot aren't."

"You said he nearly got himself killed . . ."

"That's right. Roaming the street one evening, he went around a corner and found the young woman he was smitten with, uh, plying her trade in the most crude way behind the freight office. It sent him into a fury and he attacked the man, who fought back. Timothy is no fighter, as you might guess, and the man beat him senseless, and nearly to death. The young woman—I will not call her a lady—who was at the center of it all didn't lift a finger to intervene . . . too busy lifting her skirts, I suppose. Fortunately the man desisted before it was too late for Timothy, and the boy survived. The soiled dove left Hangtree and found some other town to ruin her life in. And the lives of others, too, I'm sure."

"Very sad. I'll bid you good day now, Mrs. Bewley, and will be back to see you soon."

The front door rattled and two hefty ranch wives came in, clomping hard on the floor in pairs of manly boots probably cast off by their husbands. While Myrtle greeted the newcomers, Julia slid out the door, keeping her eyes turned away from where Timothy stood watching across the street, hoping that maybe shyness would keep him where he was and she could escape without an encounter. It didn't happen that way. Timothy was at her side, calling her "Miss Julia" before she'd gotten thirty feet from the dress shop.

"Hello, Timothy. Are you well today?"

"I'm fine, Miss Julia. Fine and good. What about you?"

"I'm quite well. Do you like my new shawl?"

"It's pretty, ma'am. Pretty like you are."

"Thank you!"

"I got you a flower. It's just made out of paper, but I hope you like it. We have them at the Emporium. I think they look real nice." He thrust the cheap item forward with an awkward smile.

"It's lovely, Timothy!" She accepted it with a smile of her own. "It's a nice thing for a friend to receive a flower from another friend. Though I don't want you to think you need to give me gifts for any reason."

"I *want* to give you gifts, Miss Julia. Because I . . . I like you. You're kind and good."

"I will treasure this flower. I'll put it up on the mirror in my room. But you work hard for your money, and I think you should spend it on yourself and your mother."

"All right, Miss Julia. All right."

"I'll be going on now, Timothy. Do you work today?"

"Yes, ma'am. I got to sweep nearly every day. Texas is a mighty dusty place, and folks tromp up and down them steps and I got to sweep them all the time."

"Hard work never really reaches its end, does it?" she said, and began to step away. Timothy watched her go and wished he had the gift of talking to females in a way that interested them. He knew his mind was slow, and he suffered greatly in most conversations, lacking things to say. Sometimes he saved up items to share that he thought might interest others . . . and one came to his mind as Julia walked away.

He hesitated only a moment, then ran after her. "Wait, Miss Julia, wait!"

She turned and frowned at him before she could stop herself. "Timothy? I'm sorry . . . I thought we'd finished talking."

"There was just something I heard about, and thought you might not have heard. Everybody's talking about it."

"Tell me, then."

"Did you hear about the dead man Sam Heller found on the road into town? Him and some other man, a stranger."

"No, I've not heard . . ."

"The dead man was an outlaw. He'd been shot dead by somebody, right through the brow's what I heard."

"How dreadful! An outlaw, you said?"

Timothy could tell that he'd authentically interested her this time. He knew that most people who talked to him were merely humoring him because they felt sorry for him. "Yes, ma'am. An outlaw name of . . . of . . ." His mind blanked.

"Can you not remember, Timothy? I'd really like to know."

"His name was . . . oh, I can't recollect it." He paused, thinking hard. "But wait . . . I do remember that they were saying he was somebody who has a brother that looks just like him. They're kind of famous, I think."

"A brother . . . a twin?"

"That's what I heard a man saying to another man while they went past me going into the Emporium."

"Toleen? Might that have been the name?"

Timothy lightly slapped his fingers against the side of his head as his memory was refreshed. "That's right! Toleen was his name. I remember now that you said it. But how'd you know?"

"Well . . . it's like you said, Timothy. They are famous outlaws."

"Outlaws are bad," Timothy said. "I don't like them."

"Some are worse than others, Timothy."

"You know outlaws, Miss Julia?"

She waved dismissively, giving no verbal answer, and made a show of admiring the paper flower he'd given her. "Thank you again for this dear gift, Timothy. You are a good friend. But now I have to be going."

"Good-bye, then, Miss Julia. I reckon I'll see you later on."

"I'll look for you every time I go to the Emporium."

"I'll look for you, too."

"Good-bye, Timothy. Have a wonderful day."

"You, too, ma'am."

"Timothy, you're sure that the name was Toleen?"

"That's what I heard."

"But his first name . . ."

"Don't know, Miss Julia. Maybe Sheriff Barton knows. I can go find him and ask him for you, if you'd like me to."

"No need for that, Timothy. It's not really important. Good day."

"Good day to you, Miss Julia."

CHAPTER SEVEN

They buried the slain outlaw in a grave on Boot Hill, near the Hangtree Church, and stuck in a cross with no name but Toleen written upon it, because no one knew which of the infamous Toleen brothers this one was. No one grieved the loss of the man because neither Toleen brother had done anything but bad with his life. Losing one was as good as losing the other.

With the dead outlaw in the ground, the only hope of identifying him lay in either finding and knowing his brother, living or dead, thus identifying this one at the same time, or in identifying the slain man through the death photograph made by Otto Perkins. That image, with some of the more gruesome facial damage obscured, had been placed on display in the Dog Star Saloon in the hope that someone would come along who knew the Toleen brothers and how to distinguish between them. Then the name on the crossbar of the Boot Hill grave marker could be completed.

So far no such identifier had appeared, so the unpleasant visage of the dead man's damaged face stared out with bird-pecked eyes across the rough-edged patrons of the Dog Star, silently pleading to be given back his missing name, and perhaps to have his killer exposed and named as well. There appeared to be little prospect of that happening. After saloon patrons became accustomed to the unsightly portrait, it ceased to be noticed or discussed. It was simply there, like a curtain in a window or a knothole in the planks of the floor.

Otto Perkins, meanwhile, had changed his usual nomadic pattern of doing business and set up a shop in a studio in Hangtree. He'd found and rented, for a three-month term, an empty shop building on the north end of town. He had moved his mobile darkroom off the wagon and into a back corner of the building, then advertised that he was available to take family portraits, wedding portraits, baby pictures, and images of corpses of the recently deceased. Over a few days he began to find work, discovering that isolated ranching families were keenly cognizant of their isolation and the fact that the lives they lived were prone to being forgotten. Portraits of families lined up before their unpainted ranch houses came into demand in Hangtree County. Newlywed couples showed up at the door of Perkins's studio, ready to pose woodenly with the young wife in a curve-backed chair and her husband in a suit he'd probably not wear again until it was time to attend a family funeral, standing sentinel-like beside her with a rigid jaw and locked knees.

The most promising development, from Perkins's perspective, was when clusters of cowboys and ranch hands from the surrounding cattle country began showing up, bearing armaments enough for a small army and various props of their line of work, such as lariats and spurs and chaps, so that they could show the present-and-future world, via photographic record, what dashing hombres they were as young men, and how deeply they had woven themselves into the warp and woof of the American West. They typically spent more than they could afford, dipping even into their whoring and drinking funds, to make sure they could obtain sufficient tin copies for their families back East to display on walls and mantels. Perkins gladly took their money, but knew these initial fees were only the beginning of what he could make on these authentic cattle country images. Shops and parlors back in the eastern cities would pay dearly for these romantic icons of the nation's frontier, especially if Perkins passed them off as pictures of outlaws, something he was quite willing to do. There was money to be made, immediately and later.

He'd just finished photographing a group of three fresh-faced youthful ranch hands, complete with peach-fuzz whiskers they'd stained with acorn juice to make them show up better, when Julia Canton came to his door. With her was Johnny Cross.

Perkins's response to the vision that was Julia Pepperday Canton was the same as that of most timid men who saw her for the first time: he was stunned silent by her beauty and simply gazed at her. Being the humble physical specimen he was, he felt pathetic and meager as she advanced toward him. But he thrust out his chin and did his best to mask his timidity.

"Good day, ma'am, sir," he said, hating the piping tenor of his own voice. Julia stared, unspeaking, while Johnny Cross said hello to the photographer.

"How may I help you?" Perkins asked.

"Howdy, sir," Johnny Cross said. "Name's Cross. Johnny Cross. I came in here looking for somebody. Jimbo Hale, man who works down at the feed store. He ain't there at the moment. You seen him?"

"I wouldn't likely know . . . I'm not familiar with the man."

As Perkins answered, an odd look shadowed across Julia's lovely features, and she stepped slightly behind Johnny Cross, putting him between herself and Perkins and pretending to look around the room, keeping her face mostly turned away from Perkins.

"Well, a gent down the street said he thought he saw Jimbo coming in here just a few minutes ago, so that's why I'm here. I'm thinking of buying an Arkansas toothpick knife he's trying to sell."

"I had some young cowboys in here to get a

photograph made, but I don't know if one of them was the man you're looking for."

"Wouldn't have been any of them. Jim Hale's three hundred pounds or more, and above forty years old. Not likely to be mistook for a young cowboy."

The front door opened and closed behind Cross. Julia had just surreptitiously exited the shop. Cross glanced over his shoulder, puzzled she had abandoned him here.

"Mr. Cross," Perkins asked, "can you tell me who that young woman is?"

"Her name's Julia Pepperday Canton. Came here from Georgia real recent. Mighty pretty young woman, as I figure you noticed. Everybody does."

"Canton?"

"That's right."

"You are certainly right regarding her beauty. Rather breathtaking, I must say." He paused, thinking hard. "Are you sure, though, about her name?"

"I got no cause to believe her name is other than what she says it is. Why? You know her as somebody else?"

"I believe I have seen her before, yes. But just where, that I can't say. In my line of work I see very many faces and hear very many names."

"And some of them are bound to resemble one another, I'd think," Cross replied.

"I can't dispute that." Perkins looked across

Johnny Cross's shoulder and through the panes in the top half of the door. The lovely lady was still out there, apparently waiting for Cross to come out. Perkins struggled to remember where he might have seen such a face before, but could not.

Cross leaned in closer and scrutinized Perkins intently. "Know what, sir? I believe maybe I've run across *you* before."

And at that moment Perkins knew with a jolt that it was true. Cross was correct: they had met. And Perkins knew exactly where and when. This fellow Johnny Cross had been among the pistol fighters Perkins had photographed along with the infamous Bloody Bill Anderson, Confederate guerrilla. There was a certain keenness in his gaze that made him memorable, along with the fact that Cross bore a resemblance to Anderson himself, though the latter was whiskered while Cross was clean-shaven both then and now. It was actually Cross's face that Perkins's eye was drawn to each time he looked at that old photograph of Anderson and his pistol fighters.

Perkins wasn't about to mention any of those details here and now, however. Anderson and his men were considered murdering criminals by much of the nation, and despite his and Cross's shared Confederate background, Perkins didn't know if Cross's affiliation with so controversial a wartime figure was something generally known. Best to just hold silent.

What Cross said next revealed he was experiencing some memories of his own.

"You took photographs during the war, I recall," Cross said. "Some of them up in Kansas and Missouri."

"I . . . I did. Is that where you saw me?"

"Don't really matter where it was. It's just interesting that we've crossed paths before. And that you believe you also saw the same lady I'm walking about town with today."

"As they say, it's a small world."

"You betcha. Let me call her in and see if she might remember you, too."

"Please, sir, don't. She stepped outside so there must be some reason she did not want to be in here. Perhaps she just needed fresh air."

"Whatever you say. I don't know about the fresh air, though. To me Hangtree air always smells like dust and horse poop."

Perkins gave an obligatory chuckle. "Mr. Cross, let me ask you, if you don't mind: Do you and the lovely lady have a, er, formal association? Are you her beau?"

"We have no such understanding with each other. I have befriended her as a newcomer to town, mostly because, to tell the truth, I think she's the prettiest gal I've ever run across. But from what time we've spent together, I don't know that she's looking for anything more than a walking-around-town kind of man friend right now. If she ever wants more, I'm sure 'nough available for it."

Perkins merely nodded.

"Are you interested in getting to know her yourself?" Cross asked.

Perkins seemed instantly discomfited, even embarrassed. "Sir . . . this isn't the easiest thing for me to say, but let me ask you to just, well, look at me. See me? How I look? How I speak? High voice, neck the size of your wrist, stick legs and big feet. I see you struggling not to laugh, sir. Don't worry over it. I learned to laugh at myself a long time ago."

"What's your point?"

"My point is, can you imagine a man like me thinking that such a divine creature as your beautiful friend could ever see me as anything but a walking joke? I could never ask any respectable woman to look at me in a serious way. Why would she want to?"

"You're mighty hard on yourself, friend."

"Mr. Cross, there is no way a man of your appearance and appeal could possible understand life as a man like me experiences it. You enter a room and every eye turns your way and smiles brighten the faces of every female. The same usually happens to me, but for very different, even opposite, reasons. Any woman who smiles at me does it out of amusement."

Cross did his best to look encouraging and clapped his hand on the photographer's shoulder and gripped firmly. "Sir, sir, I can tell you with absolute truthfulness that I've seen much lesser specimens than you end up with women you would never imagine taking so much as a glance their way. What you believe about yourself, other folks are going to believe, too, in the end. If you look on yourself the way you described just now, you got no chance of having other people, women most of all, seeing the better side of you."

"How can I help it? I mean . . . look at me! That woman out there sees you, she sees a handsome face and strong arms and a man able to fight his fights and maybe hers too. Me, she sees a little bug of a man who can take a picture of her and . . . and . . . well, in my case, that's about it."

"Hold on a minute."

Johnny Cross went to the door and opened it. Julia Canton looked at him with expectation and welcome, obviously ready to move on down the street. But Cross instead motioned her to come back inside with him.

Her reluctance to do so was evident and confusing. Cross gave her a quizzical look and motioned again for her to come. She did, and entered the photographer's business with a downcast face, simply refusing to look at the little man behind the counter.

Cross said, "Julia, I want you to do me a favor. Shake Mr. Perkins's hand here and tell him to cheer up. Coming from you I think that would go a long way."

She slowly raised her head, her manner strange and nervous. Johnny Cross looked from her to Perkins and back again, trying to decide which of the two was the more unsettled. Perkins's situation he could understand, but Julia's was incomprehensible.

"Julia?"

"I need to go," she said, still looking down. "I'm . . . unwell. Feeling poorly."

"Oh. We'll go right now, then." He grinned at Perkins. "If Jim Hale comes back in here, tell him Johnny Cross wants to talk to him about that knife."

"I will."

As she and Cross turned to leave, Julia took a fast glance at Perkins, giving him his clearest look at her. She wheeled and was gone.

When the door closed behind her and Johnny Cross, Perkins went back to a rear corner of his thrown-together place of business. A chest in which he stored volumes of his photographic work over the years, labeled and indexed. He opened the chest and dug out a particular volume, which he carried up to the counter. No customers were present. He opened the heavy, thick volume, referenced dates marked on the tops of the leafs, and found a particular image, which he studied closely.

He closed the volume and put it on a shelf beneath the counter. Returning to the chest, he dug in deeper and pulled out an older volume of images. This one he studied more slowly, with the help of a magnifying glass. Finding at last the picture he sought, he examined it until he was satisfied that his memory had been confirmed.

What really intrigued him was a sense that he was beginning to see connections where they seemed unlikely to exist. He wasn't sure he had seen enough to identify an undeniable pattern yet . . . but the coincidences intrigued him.

Something was happening in this cursed little town. Otto Perkins could feel it in his bones.

CHAPTER EIGHT

"Want it back, half-wit? Come get it, then! Here it is!"

The red-haired man with a face ruined by too many years of Texas sun chortled maliciously and tossed Timothy Holt's flop hat high over the young man's head and into the hands of another man whose laugh was just as harsh. Timothy leaped high, hands lifted, but the hat was a yard or more beyond his reach. He landed clumsily, stumbled, and twisted his ankle as he fell off the boardwalk in front of Lockhart's Emporium. Timothy yelped in pain and fell to the dirt, which was mostly mud at the moment because of horse urine.

The two men, strangers in Hangtree, roared in mocking laughter as the mentally slow young man made sounds of disgust at having been sullied in such an unpleasant way. "What's the matter, boy?" the first abuser asked. "You don't like making mud pies, half-wit?"

"Why, Hiram," said the second man, who still held Timothy's hat, "I'd think that any half-wit fool would like to play in mud, you know, being just a child in his mind!"

"That's right, Bill! He ought to be having himself a good time! Make us a good mud pie there, dummy! Maybe eat it for us!"

"You men, you should leave that poor fellow alone!" a woman said, coming out of the Emporium with a well-laden basket of goods on her arm. "He can't help that he's a fool!"

Timothy was at that moment trying to get up, but the pain in his twisted ankle stabbed him and he put his foot down too fast, slipping in the mud-urine mix and twisting the ankle a second time. He sent up a howl that could have been heard on the far side of town.

A well-dressed stranger, who had just come from the saloon where the picture of the slain Toleen brother stood on its easel, looking out at saloon patrons through eye sockets rendered hollow by hungry buzzards, leaned against a hitchrail on down the street a few dozen yards, and watched the performance in front of the big general store with what seemed only meager interest. A closer look at him, though, would have revealed that his eyes never veered away from the activity, even when he pulled makings from a pocket and rolled a quirly with experienced fingers.

Bill threw the flop hat over Timothy again and back to Hiram. Timothy this time made no effort to intercept the hat, being too distracted by ankle

pain. Hiram moved forward, holding out the
hat toward the young man as if about to give it
to him. Timothy, aware he was being toyed with,
hesitantly reached out to take it, but Hiram
yanked it back and with a laugh threw it back to
Bill. They were like two mean boys in a school-
yard picking on their weakest schoolmate. Bill,
moving fast, went to where Timothy was, swept
the hat down into the puddle of mud, then
pushed the fouled thing down onto Timothy's
head. He and his partner laughed heartily.

The woman with the basket could handle it no
more. She dropped the basket, crossed the boardwalk, and with fist balled, pounded Bill on the side
of his head, hard enough to make him slip on the
side of the boardwalk much as Timothy had, and
fall into the urine-infused mud beside him.

The silent, smoking stranger who watched it
all from down the street chuckled as he drew
deeply on his cigarette.

She wasn't through yet. She stepped into the
street, reached down and hauled up a handful of
mud, and stormed toward Hiram, who had begun
the torment of Timothy in the first place. Hiram,
a foot and a half taller than the woman and nearly
twice her weight, put up a hand to block her.
She dodged athletically and managed to shove
enough mud into Hiram's mouth to nearly fill it.
He accidentally inhaled some of it into his throat,
and went into a coughing frenzy so intense he
almost heaved. Sputtering and with mud washing
down his chin, he shoved the woman away and

down, getting upright and stumbling away from her and Timothy as well. His companion, Bill, watched Hiram's actions in a mix of surprise, alarm, and laughter. The handful of others on the street and boardwalk were laughing, too, and Hiram reddened when he realized it.

Hiram Tate could not bear to be laughed at.

Smeared with mud, reeking of horse urine, and with dirt-flecked spittle flying from his cursing mouth, Hiram rampaged about, roaring out his anger like some rabid beast. The woman who had humiliated him, equally befouled, also got to her feet. Hiram moved at her with a yell, scaring her badly and making her stagger back against the boardwalk's edge. She wavered but somehow avoided falling.

The small pistol the woman suddenly held in her hand had seemingly come from nowhere. Only Timothy Holt had seen her pull it from a pocket sewn into the side of her skirt. He watched as the woman thumbed back the hammer and aimed it at Hiram's livid, grimy face. Hiram himself didn't seem to notice the gun, or so it appeared to Timothy, because he advanced onward, quite fast, cursing the woman foully.

"Hiram!" shouted Bill, who saw that his partner was fast losing control of his actions, compelled by a blind rage and wounded dignity. And the woman was so terrified there was no predicting what she might do with that gun, intentionally or otherwise. This would not end well.

So Bill intervened, joining the fray and trying to somehow bring an end to it. With the advantage of surprise, he was able to get a hold on the little pistol and wrench it out of the woman's hand. He held it back and aloft, out of her reach, and back-stepped onto the boardwalk and toward the store building, laughing with triumph.

And then it was gone. The pistol was taken from his own hand just as fast as he had taken it from the woman's. With a muttered oath, Bill wheeled and saw that Timothy had the pistol now. Bill was washed over with embarrassment . . . outwitted by a simpleton! Hiram Tate would never let him hear the end of it.

"Boy, you hand me that pistol back, you hear?" Bill held out his hand and tried to look intimidating.

Timothy would have none of it. The pistol in his hand gave him a sense of power he was not accustomed to. He waved the weapon in Bill's direction and took two steps back. "I'll shoot you!" Timothy declared loudly.

The pistol moved about in such a broad pattern that it was clear to all watching that Timothy might hit anything or anyone within a 180-degree sweep, if the pistol went off. People ran for cover or to put themselves beside or behind Timothy.

"You don't want to shoot nobody, boy," said Bill, still advancing, nervously. Timothy, visibly quaking, was so scared and antagonized that it was possible he really would shoot, even if only by accident.

"Do what he says, boy," Hiram said from the street. Timothy, afraid to look fully away from Bill, even so flicked his eyes half a second toward Hiram and saw that the big man had a pistol of his own. He'd drawn it and it was now leveled directly at Timothy. Hiram's gun hand was not shaking. "Drop that pistol, half-wit."

The woman who had intruded herself into the situation, and whose pistol was now in Timothy's hand, wailed loudly in tension and fear. Her banshee-like cry unsettled Hiram a little, and he glanced away from Timothy . . .

. . . and saw a man with long yellow hair striding toward him with a sawed-off rifle in his hand, bandolier belts draping his shoulders and chest, and a look on his face that put Hiram in danger of losing control of his bladder right where he stood.

Beyond the advancing man Hiram saw another man, leaning on a tierail and smoking a cigarette. He paid little heed to the man, the yellow-haired man dominating his attention.

"Down with the pistol, you!" Sam Heller said, punctuating the command by lifting the chopped-down rifle an inch or two higher, so that if he fired, the slug would tear through Hiram's intestines somewhere between navel and groin.

"That dummy is threatening my partner with that pistol he stole!" Hiram answered. "Hell, he's a public menace! A danger to us all! It's *him* you ought to disarm."

"Timothy is as gentle a soul as you'll find anywhere in the Pecos country," Heller replied, moving his mule-leg up another little bit.

"Timothy," Heller said, "best you run that pistol up into the store and leave it with Mr. Lockhart. There's no call for you to need to hurt anybody or to get hurt yourself. You don't want that."

"Yes, sir, Mr. Sam," Timothy said, and headed for the Emporium's front door.

Long-trained instincts told Heller that the big man with the pistol would likely try to take advantage of the minor distraction of Timothy's movement to make a move of his own. Though Heller didn't know Hiram Tate, he knew something about him, something the former Pinkerton had learned to read in others with little more than a glance. Everything in the pistoleer's manner, stance, and expression told Heller that Tate carried in him a dangerous pride that would not let him tolerate being bested or publicly shamed. This was the kind of man, with the kind of pride, that turned minor brawls into deadly fights. Heller's hand tightened on the grip of the mule-leg rifle.

Hiram Tate swung and was about to fire at Heller when Heller's weapon spoke first. With a blast akin to cannon fire, a hot slug left the shortened rifle and hit Tate right where Heller intended: the joint of his left shoulder. Tate grunted, spun, and fell, staining the ground red. His left arm was very nearly shot off, the joint shattered, the ball torn out of the socket, and only ragged flesh keeping the appendage attached to Tate's body.

Tate writhed and screamed, dropping the pistol from his right hand and groping across his chest at his ruined shoulder. Blood poured between his twitching fingers.

Heller walked over to the fallen man and kicked his dropped pistol up under the boardwalk, out of reach. He leaned over a little and poked at Tate's shoulder wound with the hot, short muzzle of the mule-leg. Tate screamed even louder, and his partner, Bill, a much less hardy man, stumbled to one side and vomited over the back side of the boardwalk.

"You said something about 'disarming' somebody," Heller said. "Now you know how *I* 'disarm' a man."

"God, I'm hurting, I'm hurting . . ." The redhaired Hiram's groans were pathetic.

"I bet you are. But you should thank me, really. I could have shot you in the gut, or the belly, or the heart or face. I was in a kindhearted humor today, though. I could see you weren't a lefty because of which hand your pistol was in. So I decided that if you had to lose an arm, I'd at least let it be the left one, which you wouldn't need as much."

"Oh God . . . God . . . you expect me to *thank* you for blowing my arm off?"

"I expect you to get up and quit bloodying up the street, and to let me haul you off to the local sawbones and get that arm off the rest of the way, good and clean. Otherwise it's going to just mortify on you and rot off, and probably by the time it was ready to fall off of its own weight, you'd have died from blood poisoning anyway. Look there, you fool! With all that twisting around, you've ground the wound right into the dirt. It'll be dripping rot and pus in no time. Yep, you'd best get that flop arm hacked off right, or get ready to die hard and slow. Death by mortification ain't no way for a man to go. I've seen it before. You don't want it."

Heaving and coughing noises from Bill over on the boardwalk, on his knees, let Heller know that he was going to be no threat. But still he had an interest in the fellow. Something about him seemed familiar.

Lockhart the merchant, helped by a store clerk, came out of the Emporium carrying a wooden door. This became a makeshift stretcher for Hiram Tate, who was fast on his way to the local doctor for an amputation already mostly completed courtesy of Sam Heller's mule-leg rifle.

CHAPTER NINE

Though the slug from Heller's mule-leg had struck no vital organs, and blood loss had been sufficiently controlled to keep Hiram Tate from bleeding to death, Hiram died on the doctor's table anyway.

His heart, defective without anyone knowing it, including Hiram himself, was too taxed by the stress of his injuries to survive its ordeal. It simply shut down and the physician tending him found himself suddenly working to amputate the arm of a dead man. No point in that, he figured, so he stopped, washed himself up, and had Hiram hauled off to the local undertaker with both arms still in place, though the shot one was barely hanging on.

The doctor, who typically took a few nips before taking a knife to anyone, leaned unsteadily over the dead man, then asked Heller, "Who is this poor joker?"

"I don't know, but I know I've seen him before. Kind of like that dead man I and that new picture-taker man found out on the Hangtree Road t'other day. Something familiar about him."

"I had the same notion myself," the doctor said. "But I can't put a finger on . . . wait a minute. Wait. I think I know."

Someone knocked on the outer office door, then immediately opened it. Sheriff Mack Barton walked in and stepped into the treatment room where the surgery had been taking place. "Doc, howdy. You, too, Heller. Heard about what happened. How's the man who got . . . oh. I can see for myself. What did you do, Heller? Gut-shoot him?"

"Nope. Just that left shoulder. No reason he should have died that I can see."

"Well, dead he is, anyway. And it really don't matter . . . the reward for this one is on a dead-or-alive basis."

"So I was right," the doctor said. "I knew I'd seen this man's face before."

"Wanted poster?" Heller asked.

"That's right," the doctor replied. "I was in over at Sheriff Barton's office just a week ago . . . remember, Sheriff? You had that toenail growing into your toe and I had to cut it out?"

"God, yes, I remember, and I got to tell you, Doc, you missed your calling. Should have been a butcher, the way you hacked on me."

"Feels better now, though, don't it? And I can

tell you there's not been much difference between medicine and butcher work since the war. If I had ten cents for every arm and leg I sawed off during that damn war, I'd not have to be feeding potions and pills to a gang of Texas plains-hoppers."

Heller waved his hand over the dead man. "So, who is he?"

"Well, at one time he was right-hand man to none other than Black Ear Skinner himself," said Barton. "Hiram Tate. Wanted here, over in Arkansas, all the way down into Louisiana, and north of here clear into Kansas. Bad apple, this one was."

"Didn't show a dang lot of sense, making such a show of himself on a public street with him being wanted everywhere," Heller said. "All just to poke fun at a feeble-minded fellow."

"These type of men ain't generally smart," said Barton. "This one made it far as he has without getting himself killed more by luck than keen wits. But he has brought *you* some luck, Heller: he's got reward money on his head, and since it was your bullet that brought him down, you got it coming to you."

"How much?"

"Don't recall right off. It's on the Wanted notice. Good likeness of this gent, too. Good enough that it really looks like him. A lot of them pictures, hell, they could be about anybody."

"Tell you what, Mack, I want that money to be given to the Hangtree Church. They got a steeple that's going to blow down flat in the next stout wind. Let Preacher Fulton use that reward, whatever it is, to get that steeple in good shape."

"Mighty big of you to do that, Sam."

"I don't need the money. I got aplenty of it. Not saying it to brag, just stating the fact."

"The reverend and his congregation are going to be mighty grateful."

"Like I said, I don't really need it myself. Might as well do some good for the town with it."

"I got some improvements that could be made at the jail," Barton said.

"Can't solve every problem myself," Heller said. "I'll stick with the church for this one." He looked down at the pallid-but-freckled face of the red-haired corpse. "One of the Black Ear gang, huh? Mighty strange, considering that the dead man out on the Hangtree Road was one of the Black Ears himself. And that old fellow who got his teeth knocked out by that pretty young lady in Sunday services awhile back . . . his name was Josiah Enoch, and I heard it said over at the Cattleman Hotel that he had some connection with the Black Ears, too, going back quite a few years."

"Makes a man wonder," Barton commented. "Why is it everybody coming into town lately has ties to Black Ear Skinner, may he rot in hell?"

"I've wondered the same myself, even before this one here came along," Heller said, indicating the dead man lying supine before them. "It's a mighty odd coincidence, no question about it. Why would folks associated with an outlaw who's been dead for five years all at once show up in such an out-of-the-way place as Hangtree?"

"No idea," said Barton. "But I don't like it. Puts me on edge."

"Amen to that," said Heller. "Seems like the only newcomer to Hangtree lately who ain't tied in with the Black Ear gang is that pretty woman who knocked that man's teeth out in church."

"She's been going about town with Johnny Cross, you know," said Barton.

"That's only because she ain't had the chance to meet me yet," replied Heller, and grinned.

The man named Bill Creed who had joined the late Hiram Tate in tormenting Timothy Holt turned out to have a Wanted poster of his own, but with a relatively miniscule award attached. There was no known connection in his case to the infamous and allegedly defunct Black Ear gang beyond the fact he had traveled to Hangtree with Hiram Tate. Quizzed closely by Barton as to what had led Tate to come to Hangtree at all, and whether Bill had any knowledge of why the other dead Black Ear, Toleen, had come to Hangtree as well, Bill Creed professed no knowledge of either matter.

Barton, alone in the jail with Bill Creed, who was chained to a chair, pulled a gleaming knife from a sheath and pressed the tip directly beside Creed's Adam's apple, hard enough to barely break the skin. A small red drop trickled down Creed's neck.

Barton's voice was a snarl. "Listen to me, you dog: I'm the sheriff of this county, and this is one sheriff who gets mighty nervous when members of one of the foulest criminal gangs on this side of the nation start turning up in his county. We've got one of the Toleen brothers rotting in his grave on Boot Hill, killed by God-only-knows-who while he was heading toward this town. We've got your partner Hiram, a known Black Ear, causing trouble in our streets and getting himself killed. And we had an old fellow who used to be a Black Ear years ago trying to rob a Sunday morning church congregation. Ever heard of such a thing? Bothers me to see such things happening in my county and my town. But you know what really bothers me about it all, Mr. Creed? Do you?"

"N . . . no, Sheriff. I don't."

"It bothers me that every one of them folk are tied to Black Ear Skinner. Every one! Makes me want to know why!"

"I don't know, sheriff. I don't. I rode with Hiram, I don't deny it, but there ain't no crime in just traveling with a man. And Hiram wasn't no member of the Black Ear gang lately . . . Black Ear Skinner has been dead for years now. Shot down in the town of Mason during a stagecoach robbery. Bled to death in the dirt. Hiram saw it with his own eyes. After that the Black Ears scattered out and there wasn't no gang no more. Still ain't, far as I know."

"You seem to know a good deal about Black Ear business, Mr. Creed."

"Just what Hiram told me, that's all. Hiram was the Black Ear, not me. I'm just a common old man of the road, that's all."

"Um-hmm. A common old man of the road who robbed two freight offices in Arkansas, shot up a dance hall in San Antonio, and beat up an old Cherokee man up in the Nations."

"Sheriff, I know I've done wrong things and broke laws. But I swear to you, swear right on a Bible if you want me to, that if you'll let me go from here you'll never see me in your county again, nor hear of me doing no more law-breaking. Not anywhere. I'll give it all up and be as good a man as you'll find. I swear it. Just give me a chance, Sheriff Barton. I beg you."

"Mr. Creed, you're the kind of man who has had chance after chance already, and pissed away every one of them. I got no reason to think you've got any good inside you. I don't believe a man like you can follow the law. It's in your blood and bone to break every rule you run across. You can moan and swear and repent and make all the promises you want to me here today, but I believe that if I let you go out that door and get on your horse and ride, before sundown tomorrow you'd have robbed some poor old farmer or cattleman, and stole the pie cooling in some widow woman's window. Then you'd be on to the next town and doing it all again."

"I won't, sir. I swear I won't."

"I'll hold you to that, friend. I want you to ride out of this town and this county, and I don't want to see you back here again. We don't need more of your kind in Hangtree."

"Sheriff, I'll be more than happy to leave this place. It's been nothing but trouble for me."

"What were you doing in company with such a man as Hiram Tate, anyway? That man had ties to some bad folk. Real bad."

"I know. I should have stayed clear of him. But I didn't. I let whiskey lure me. He was willing to buy and I was willing to drink with him, and after that I just ended up riding with him a spell. I shouldn't have done it. I knew he was a no-'count man."

"Worse than that. He was part of the Black Ear bunch, you know it? You'll not run across fouler scoundrels than them devils. And dear departed Hiram ain't the only Black Ear we've had show up hereabouts lately. One of the Toleen brothers was found shot dead out on the road into town. An old-timer from Black Ear's earlier days actually tried to rob our local churchgoers on a Sunday morning, right in church. Spunky gal visiting the service knocked his teeth down his gullet with a wooden collection plate for his trouble."

"The hell!"

"Got me right worried, these Black Ears drifting in here."

"If I was a sheriff, it'd worry me, too," Bill said. "I can't deny it."

"Did you know any others of the Black Ears besides Hiram Tate?"

"No, I didn't. Didn't know Hiram all that well or all that long."

"Did he ever talk about the Toleen brothers?"

"Mentioned them only once I can remember. Said they didn't get along with each other very well."

"Maybe our dead Toleen was kilt by his own brother, then."

"Maybe."

"Let me just ask you straight-out: Mr. Creed, do you have any notion, even a good guess, why old members of Black Ear Skinner's gang might be congregating theirselves in and around Hangtree, Texas?"

"Well, sir, I don't know how I would know such a thing, and I'd be not much inclined to try to guess," Bill Creed said. He risked a small joke. "Maybe Black Ear's boys are getting together to set up a school for poor Comanche children. You reckon?"

"Not likely, Mr. Creed. Not likely."

Sheriff Barton arched his back and winced as his spine made an audible pop. His gut rumbled just as loudly right after.

"Mr. Creed, sir, a minute ago you said something about how you wish I'd just let you walk out of here and leave our happy little community. Well, you know I can't do that. But I'll tell you something, and you can figure for yourself how you want to deal with it."

"Uh-huh," muttered an obviously puzzled Bill Creed.

"Sir, this old sheriff needs to pay a visit to the outhouse out behind the courthouse. Now, from the noise my gut is making and the messages it's sending me, I can tell you I can't dawdle around long before I make that visit. So I'm going to put you on your honor here and leave you sitting right here while I go tend to the needs of my gut. Now, there's a knothole or two in the privy walls that a man can see out of if he's squatted on the hole, but none where I could see anybody coming or going from where we are right now. So even though a law-respecting sheriff can't give a prisoner permission to walk out of a jail, the fact is, for the next few minutes I ain't going to know if, say, you lit up from where you're setting there and headed out the side door. I ain't suggesting you do that, for if you do I'll have no choice but to write you up as an escapee . . . but I'm just saying that if you did do it, I'd not even know about it before you had time to scratch a good bit of gravel." The sheriff's intestines grumbled and gurgled again, even louder, and he put a hand to his abdomen. "Well, there ain't no more waiting. I'm heading for the outhouse, and I'll leave you to think about what I just said. But if I was you I wouldn't think too long. I'll be in that outhouse awhile, but not forever. And my deputy—Clifton

Smalls is his name, big tall beanpole of a feller—
he'll be back here any time now."

"Sheriff, you leaving me free to walk out?"

"You're my prisoner. You ain't allowed to just
walk out. But an open door is an open door.
Know what I'm saying, Mr. Creed?"

"Why, Sheriff?"

"Hell, even a good lawman can forget to close
and lock a door behind him . . . especially when
he's about to mess his own britches. No more
time to talk, sir. I'll be in the outhouse if you
need me. Just one last thing, in case this is my
final chance to say it: Next time you're in a town
and you see some poor half-wit sweeping the
boardwalk in front of the general store, and you
get hit with a strong temptation to torment him
a little, resist it. Just look that temptation in the
eye and resist it. Gotta go now."

And he was gone, out of the room and then
out of the jail, heading for the outhouse at a
fast trot.

Bill Creed required no time at all to think
through his situation. He was out of the building
almost as fast as Sheriff Barton was, laughing in
his throat and marveling at this most unexpected
and welcome turn of events. His lucky stars had
been good to him. Mighty good.

Time to say good-bye to Hangtree, Texas.

CHAPTER TEN

Myrtle Bewley had not intended to discuss with her employee the unfortunate matter of Timothy Holt having been publicly tormented outside the Lockhart Emporium by two troublesome strangers, one of them now deceased through violence. But her new part-time clerk had mentioned it on her own. Myrtle was not one to pass up the latest town gossip, which she traded in more than in sewing thread and thimbles. Especially if someone else brought it up.

"It's disgusting, absolutely disgusting, treating a helpless fellow like Timothy in such a way! Humiliating him for the sake of some perverse idea of fun! It makes me furious!"

"I can see that," Myrtle replied to Julia Canton, who had come in asking about employment the day after her first visit to the dress shop. Myrtle suspected that Julia didn't so much need the meager pay as simply something to do with her time in a town full of strangers. Myrtle could tell from

Julia's manners, way of dress, and general bearing that she possessed some level of means and was accustomed to a comfortable standard of living. And her diction and vocabulary revealed the tracks of a good education.

None of that much mattered to Myrtle. What had led her to hire Julia was the prospect that she would stir new business, and that had proven true. Myrtle had been quite amused to see how many Hangtree men suddenly found cause to visit a dress shop, a place most had shunned in the past except for those times their wives forced them to bring them into town for fabric, thread, or a new garment. In Julia's brief tenure in the shop so far, Myrtle had seen men who possessed neither wives nor known intimate companions visiting her shop for no obvious reason beyond the chance to have a look at Julia Canton, and if they dared, to converse with her. Also amusing was the fact that female business in the shop had also increased, letting Myrtle know the women of Hangtree were well aware that there was a new standard-setter for feminine beauty in their town, and wanted to have a look for themselves at what had their men so distracted.

"People can be very hard on weak ones," Myrtle said. "Especially in country like this, where being weak is a danger. They shouldn't have been treating poor Tim that way, but that's the way people do, and it isn't something you can expect to change."

"I have . . . I had a brother who was much like

Timothy. That's why I care so much about it when the feeble-minded are mistreated."

"You are a woman with a good heart in her bosom," Myrtle said, thinking but certainly not adding aloud that it was surely Julia's bosom itself, not the heart within, that had the attention and admiration of most of Hangtree. "Nothing good in the hearts of the men who plagued the poor boy, though. I hear rumors that at least one of them used to be among the ranks of the gun-hawks who rode for none other than Black Ear Skinner, a devil if ever there was one."

Myrtle was looking out the front window of the shop as she said those words, eying a nicely dressed man who was unfamiliar to her. He was loitering on the far side of the street, slowly light-ing a cigar with a sulfur-and-phosphorus match he'd struck against a porch rail. His eyes, Myrtle noticed, flicked up occasionally to look toward the dress shop as he stretched out his tobacco-lighting as long as possible. Occupied with watch-ing the man, Myrtle did not notice the little jerk of Julia's head when she said the name of Black Ear Skinner.

"I think I've heard of him," Julia said. "An outlaw, I think?"

"The worst of them. Thank God he's dead and gone. Killed during a robbery he and his gang were committing."

Julia said nothing. Her gaze had followed Myrtle's out through the front window to study the stranger across the street.

"You know him?" Myrtle asked her employee.

"How would I know a dead outlaw?"

"I mean the man out there. He's a stranger to me."

"I've been in this town far less time than you," Julia said. "How would I possibly know him?"

"I've . . . somehow I've angered you," Myrtle said.

Julia gave one of her bright-as-daylight smiles. "Nonsense! You've done nothing to anger me at all. Why would you think that?"

"Never mind it, then. I just talk too much, that's all. Now I think I'll go put the spools of thread back in order. Somebody played fruit basket turnover with them."

"I hadn't realized it or I would have straightened it out myself," said Julia. "I'll be more aware of such things as I get used to this place and the way things are supposed to be."

"If you can straighten those bolts of cloth in the corner a bit, that would help greatly," Myrtle said.

"I'll get on it right away."

Myrtle hummed as she worked, and after ten minutes of it, Julia found it annoying. There was no prudent way to complain, however, so she forced her attention to the bolts of cloth customers had knocked awry, and mentally hummed a tune of her own to try to drown out Myrtle's off-key warbling.

A glance out the window a few moments later

revealed the man who had been lighting the cigar and watching the store was no longer there. Julia looked up and down the street as far as the window would allow, and did not see the man. For some reason either instinctive or silly, she was glad he had gone. There was no good reason to think his presence out there had anything to do with her, but the feeling was there that, in fact, it did.

Probably just another man hoping to get a look at her, Julia told herself. She'd lived long enough now as a nubile and exceptionally beautiful young woman to realize she was an inevitable leading attraction anywhere she went. It was exhausting. She knew that other women were jealous of her, and a time or two had tried to explain to some of those she counted as friends that there was little to envy in her situation. It was virtually impossible for her to know whether men who were drawn to her saw anything in her beyond her appearance. Even those whom she allowed to get to know her as a person didn't seem to care much about any aspect of her other than that which was superficial and unimportant. There were many times in her life when she had longed to move among others without drawing any attention to herself. To disappear, and reappear as someone else. Someone merely average, a face in the crowd.

Such was not possible for a female of such remarkable beauty. So Julia had learned to use her extraordinary appearance, the aspect of herself that, to her, seemed more a handicap than a benefit, to her own advantage. With a mere smile and brush of her hand, she could obtain from men what she needed and wanted. Money, praise, help in times of trouble, even physical protection. Whatever she might do in her life, she knew and accepted the fact that her true profession would be manipulation.

Even now, in this meaningless little job in a tiny dress shop in a nowhere town, a job she had sought out sheerly to avoid boredom, she was playing a manipulative game. Julia could tell that Myrtle Bewley was a woman with a certain degree of sense and acumen, enough to realize that having a lovely young woman in her shop would be good for business. She had played on that to manipulate the woman into giving her what she wanted.

Julia had just straightened the last bolt of cloth when she realized that Myrtle at last had stopped her droning humming. Yet still Julia heard music. Not humming, though, but fiddle music, and muffled to the point that she wondered if she might be imagining it. No, there it was again. Real music, coming from the direction of the back of the shop.

Myrtle came walking up and admired Julia's improvements of the display of fabric. "Looking much better," she said. Then she cocked her head and listened to the hard-to-hear fiddle music. "And Claude is sounding better this year than last, too. Improvements everywhere we look and listen!"

"Claude?"

"That's right. The fiddle music—you hear it, don't you—that's Claude Farley. He's been the resident fiddler in this town for about as long as it has been here. He taught himself, and for the first year or so his fiddling sounded a little like a screeching cat with its tail being squeezed in a clothes wringer. And that being a cat with very little ear for melody." Myrtle tilted her head a little further and nodded with the rhythm of the music. "Yes, better now, much better. Claude must have been practicing out there in that farmhouse the last couple of years."

"I can't hear him well, but he sounds fine to me," Julia said.

"Do you know him?" Myrtle asked.

"No. I'm quite sure I don't."

"I think you've probably met him and don't realize it. He lives in the same boardinghouse you're in now. You've probably dined at table with him and his wife, Hilda."

"I thought you said he lived in a farmhouse."

"He did, until it burned down at the first of the year. Complete loss. He and Hilda moved into town and rented the biggest room in the boardinghouse, and have been there ever since."

"Gray-haired man with a white-haired wife? Older folk?"

"That's them."

"I have met them, then. The names just didn't

stay with me. He's a quiet man, very little to say at the table."

Myrtle nodded and straightened some thimbles on a little shelf nearby. "That's Claude. Silent as a church mouse, except when he has his fiddle in hand."

"I haven't heard him play at the boardinghouse."

"He generally does his practicing in an old shed about an eighth of a mile out that way." She pointed toward the rear of the shop. "He's shy about his fiddling until he's practiced up."

"Why is he practicing now, I wonder?"

"You haven't heard, I guess. We've got a big dance coming up, going to be held at the big horse barn over on the south end of town. Outside if the weather is good, inside if it rains. Claude provides the music. The town's held dances every few months since the end of the war. There'll be a couple of pigs roasted in the ground and lots of steaks fried. The idea is to give people a chance to know each other better and put aside differences."

"Does it work?"

"There was a knife fight at the last two dances. Same men both times, and they were drunk both times, too."

"Oh my."

"It can be a rowdy town sometimes. It's Texas, after all."

Julia smiled. "A dance. It sounds like it could

be a pleasant diversion . . . if knife fights can be avoided."

"It will happen a week from this Friday night. I'm quite sure you'll receive plenty of invitations, being as pretty as you are. I'm surprised Johnny Cross hasn't asked you already. If he wastes too much time, he might lose his dancing partner to somebody else."

Julia gave an impish grin and shrugged. "Maybe so. Maybe Sam Heller."

"Oh! Have you met him now?"

"Well, no. But I dropped a subtle word or two with a couple of busybodies who hang around the boardinghouse, looking for gossip. Just to let him get the word that I've heard of him and have an interest in meeting him."

"Oh! Very forward of you, my dear."

"My father always taught me to say what it is you want, and not to be shy about it."

"You might want to be aware that Sam Heller and Johnny Cross have an . . . unusual kind of relationship. Mutual respect and antagonism all rolled up together until it's hard to peel the two apart."

"Well, neither man has asked me yet. Who knows? Someone else might ask me before either one of them gets around to it."

"Yes, indeedy, Julia. And speaking of that, there comes a likely prospect for asking you right now."

Julia looked out the window and felt her heart

sink as she saw, just entering the angle of view allowed by the window, Timothy Holt, walking toward the shop with another paper flower in his hand.

"It is very nice of you to ask me, Timothy," said Julia as she walked with the humble young man in what he told her was the direction of his home. "I don't know I've ever been invited to a dance by a better young man."

"So, you'll go with me?" Timothy asked, his smile bright and his step quickening.

"Timothy, it wouldn't be right of me to say yes," she said. "It would give you, I mean, give people, the wrong impression of our friendship."

"But you are my friend, right, Miss Julia?"

"Of course I'm your friend. But that is all I can be, Timothy. Just your friend."

"Well . . . can you go with me to the town dance?"

"No, Timothy. I can thank you for asking me, but I can't go with you."

Timothy's shoulders slumped and he looked down. Conversation ended for a few moments.

"Are we still going the right direction to your house?" Julia asked.

"Yes."

"May I meet your mother when we get there?"

"Yes. If you want to."

"I'd like to tell her how much I admire her son."

Timothy had nothing to say. In moments he turned down an alley and Julia followed.

The house would have been easy to pass by with barely a notice. Made in a simple rectangular pattern, no more than a shed, really, it was made of the same unpainted wood as a nearby small barn. From the outside the place looked barely large enough to accommodate two occupants.

Timothy's widowed mother was named Margaret, and a more slumped, exhausted-looking woman Julia had never seen. It was clear within moments of beginning to speak with her that Margaret Holt was nearly blind and also hard of hearing. Clearly she was not equipped to pursue a livelihood. The importance of Timothy's meager earnings made with his broom, and the charity foods sent home with him from local cafés, as Myrtle had told her about, became clear in a rush.

The only chair Margaret had to offer was a crude bench sitting against a bare and windowless side wall, near the cot that apparently served Timothy as a bed. Margaret's bed was as crudely made as a cot, but was bigger and was an authentic bed, complete with a straw-stuffed bedtick. It was the nicest item in the entire tiny house.

Julia did her best to converse with Margaret, but the woman possessed a slurring impediment of speech and Julia understood only some of what she said. What came through was Margaret's appreciation for Julia's having been kind to her son, who had spoken of Julia to Margaret with great affection.

Julia was about to thank Margaret for passing on the laudatory words when Margaret suddenly shifted her manner and told Julia, in effect, to draw no closer to her son. Her theme became one Julia had heard before, from Johnny Cross: Timothy was prone to develop fast and easy infatuations, and just like most men, the more attractive the object of the infatuation, the stronger it grew. In Timothy's case infatuations were extraordinarily intense, and when they collapsed, Timothy went through times of equally intense emotional devastation. The widow spoke it all in much cruder, struggling terms, but the content of her message was clear.

"I understand," Julia said, and was secretly glad to have stronger grounds for doing what she'd already known she must do: make Timothy understand that she could be his friend, but nothing more.

Timothy heard nothing of what his mother said to Julia, because he had left the two women alone so he could go to the back door of the Cattleman and pick up whatever leftover food the chef might have. He also sought privacy to grieve over the obvious fact that Julia did not care for him in the way he cared for her.

Timothy walked along through his usual back-alley route to the Cattleman, avoiding the street so that no one would see he was occasionally wiping tears from his eyes.

How could she not love him? She was the dearest, sweetest creature he'd ever known. And she'd been kind to him, treating him like he counted, like he meant something. How could he go on like he was, alone, after having met her?

Timothy had never felt more isolated from the world around him or more hopeless of ever finding a woman of his own. And even if he did, it wouldn't be the same. It wouldn't be *her.*

CHAPTER ELEVEN

"Oh! My God, watch where you're going!"

Timothy was startled by the harsh voice and gaping face of the man he almost ran into while rounding a corner in the dark with a basket of leftover Cattleman's food in his hand. He nearly dropped the basket. The man he'd nearly collided with stumbled off to one side and almost tripped over his own feet.

Timothy caught a strong whiff of whiskey on the man's breath. It repelled him. Timothy's late father had been a hard-drinking man, and as a small boy Timothy had earned some bruises and even scars because of his father's habits. His mother had protected him as best she could, but often that wasn't good enough. And when Timothy's father hurt him, she always tried to smooth over the situation by saying, "He's been drinking, Tim. That's why he hit you. He's been drinking, that's all."

It was only natural that Timothy had come to

despise liquor and what it did to those who abused it.

The man, a small-built fellow, corrected his stumbling and steadied himself with a hand against the nearest wall. Then he studied Timothy through the thick lenses of his spectacles.

"I know who you are," he said, tongue tangling and distorting his words. "You're that feeble-minded fellow who sweeps at the big store. Timothy, I think."

"I know you, too," Timothy answered. "You're that man who takes pictures of people."

"Otto Perkins, and pleased to meet you."

"Same, sir. But you're drunk, Mr. Perkins." Timothy surprised himself with his own boldness.

"I think maybe I am. I don't drink much, but today the temptation struck and I visited the Dog Star. I planned to drink only a little, but there's a photograph there that I made myself, a very unpleasant image of a dead man I and Mr. Sam Heller found on the road some days ago, and seeing that face looking at me off its easel was distressing enough that I drank more and more."

"My papa drank a lot. It finally kilt him. That's what my mama says it was. All I know is he went out to pee one day and dropped dead."

"Very sorry. Sad for you, I'm sure. Why are you out roaming the alleyways just now, by the way? What's that in your hands?"

"It's food. The cook down at the Cattleman Hotel shares food with me and my mama."

"I'm sure that's a big help. You can't make much money sweeping for a shopkeeper."

"No. Who sweeps at your shop?"

"Any sweeping done there is done by me. Which usually means the place stays dirty."

"I could sweep for you if you'd pay me some like Mr. Lockhart does."

At another time, Perkins would have bypassed that offer without a thought. Being uncharacteristically drunk, though, he reacted with equally uncharacteristic magnanimity. "That's a good idea, Timothy. I'd be glad for the help. Can you do it and still have time to sweep at the Emporium, though?"

Timothy foresaw no problem with seeing to the needs of both businesses, and within moments an evening's chance alleyway meeting had turned into a new opportunity for a simple man who encountered few of those.

"Want to come meet my mama, Mr. Perkins? She'd like you for hiring me."

"Will that food you got there be for sharing?"

"You . . . you can have my part of it, sir. Since you're going to let me sweep for you." Timothy gave the warmest grin he could. In the shadow-casting light from a nearby window, the grin gave Timothy a ghastly look, heightened by the puffiness of his eyes. He'd wept hard a little earlier, grieving over his rejection by Julia Canton.

"You all right, boy?" asked Perkins.

"Please, sir, don't call me boy, if you would."

"Sorry . . . Tim. Timothy. Are you all right, though?"

"Sir, I was . . . I was weeping some earlier."

"You hurt? Sick?"

"Heartbroke."

"Over what?"

"There's a lady in town, name of Canton. I thought she was a friend of mine and liked me, but she wouldn't say she'd go to the dance with me. There's a dance in town before long and I really wanted to have her go with me to it."

"Canton . . . I've seen her," Perkins said. "She was in my shop once with . . . with somebody." Perkins had been about to say the name of Johnny Cross, but despite his alcohol-dulled mind, saw prudence in not doing so. Considering that Timothy had just professed his infatuation for the woman, Timothy might get jealous and imagine he could somehow take on Johnny Cross. Timothy didn't need trouble with an old pistol fighter who once rode with Quantrill and Anderson.

"She's a mighty pretty woman, Timothy. Maybe the prettiest I've ever seen anywhere. Which means there's going to be a lot of men trying to get with her . . . you might have better luck setting your sights a little lower. Don't look sad . . . it's the same with me. Like the saying goes: I could grease up a Chinaman and pin his ears back and swallow him whole quicker than I could turn the head of somebody like Miss Canton, so I just accept things as they are. I'm not going to spend my time trying to do what can't be done."

"But I like her, Mr. Perkins. Like her a whole lot. Whole lot."

Otto Perkins smiled and put his arm around Timothy's shoulder. They began to walk, going in the direction Timothy had been moving before. "My friend, the first day you come sweep my floors for me, there's something I want to show you that may give you a different perspective of Miss Canton. You see, Tim, sometimes things ain't what they appear. And people, too. Most of all people."

Timothy had no idea what Perkins was talking about, but nodded because he'd learned that it made life easier, as a man of feeble mind, just to pretend and go along with what smarter folk said.

"She was at my house this afternoon," said Timothy. "She met my mama. She might still be there, I reckon."

Perkins halted. "Miss Canton?"

"Yes."

"If she is still there, Timothy, I think we should not go in. I have reasons for that."

Timothy, who was much less upset now than he had been earlier in the evening, found himself in agreement. They walked on toward the hidden-away shack home of the little Holt family, but the prospect of them actually entering the house seemed lessened now.

* * *

They turned a corner and came in view of the Holt shack, and noticed a man standing past it, smoking a cigar and apparently watching the little house. When he noticed Timothy and Perkins, he seemed to start a little, but a moment later took on a relaxed stance and drew deeply on his cigar. "Gentlemen," he said in a burst of thick smoke.

"Hello, sir," said Perkins.

Timothy strode up to the stranger. "Why you watching my house, mister?"

"Your house? Here?" The man nodded toward the shack.

"I remember you," Timothy said. "You were out on the street when . . . when . . ."

"I was," said the man. "I remember seeing you from across the street. I'm sorry you were treated that way. It wasn't right."

Timothy stared at the ground, silent.

Perkins asked, "Why this place, and this little house, on this night?"

"Just out for a walk and a smoke," the man said. "Name's Brody. Wilfred Brody."

"Otto Perkins. And you've already met Timothy here."

"Good to meet both of you. Good evening, gentlemen." He puffed his cigar, touched the brim of his derby hat, and walked away.

"Nice enough gent, I suppose," said Perkins. "But there's something there that just feels a little . . . odd."

Timothy said nothing. He went to the door of

his humble dwelling and put his ear to it. After listening a few moments, he said, "I think Mama's in there by herself now. Come on and let her meet you."

Perkins was in his own mind ready to go on to his own room at the rear of his photography studio, but instead he joined Timothy and went inside. When the door closed them in, the man they had met appeared again out of the dark. He stared at the house, listening and waiting, then at last whispered to himself, "Well, seems she isn't in there after all. I sure don't know how she got out without me seeing her. But don't you worry, pretty lady. I'll find you and get you back where you belong. Don't you doubt it." He walked away again, this time not to return.

CHAPTER TWELVE

Her escape had been made by way of a back door, and once out of the rough little dwelling, Julia Canton had managed to move without letting the loitering stranger out in the shadows see her. She had no idea who the man was or why he seemed to be tracking and watching her. She was, however, a young woman whose life so far had involved, three times, the fighting off of unwanted and violent carnal advances. Though no one would guess it to look at her, she often carried more hidden derringers and shivs than a traveling gambler. She knew how to use them all, and a few times had done so.

After leaving the Holt shack, she was glad to have done so before the return of Timothy. She knew she'd hurt the young man's feelings, rejecting his sweet-but-unwanted invitation to the upcoming town dance. It made her feel bad for him, but also made her not want to encounter him any more than necessary. She was glad, at

least, that Timothy's sad and invalid mother
understood her son's tendency to tie his heart-
strings to women with whom there could be no
hope of a relationship. If Mrs. Holt had resented
Julia for hurting her son's feelings, Julia would
have been greatly saddened.

She made her way through town, keeping an
eye out for the man she had detected was following her. She did not see him.

Nearing her boardinghouse, Julia heard the
faint strains of Claude Farley's fiddle, scratching
out an off-key rendition of "Soldier's Joy." Julia
paused, frowning to herself as she imagined going
back to her lonely room, suffering through an
evening of boredom while listening to an old man
practice his fiddling.

An intolerable prospect. Julia couldn't face
the thought of a lonely evening. At the very least
she had to be among people, and not the dull
residents of a boardinghouse whose idea of ex-
citement was adding honey to their cups of
coffee for sweetener. How bold! Julia rolled her
eyes heavenward and for a few moments hated
the town of Hangtree.

There were, of course, the saloons. She would
have a better chance of finding diversion there,
but there would also be the inevitable approach
of drunken men who imagined they could gain
her company and favor with their pathetic at-
tempts at being suave and appealing.

There was only one man in this town who
could appeal to her, and she had yet even to

meet him. Seen him, yes, met him, no. When that inevitable meeting came, it would be important that she make sure it happened in just the right way, so that it could lead to the right result. That was the very reason she was in this backwater place at all.

She bypassed the boardinghouse and kept walking. Though there was risk in being seen in a saloon—she'd been trying to cultivate the image of a moral, churchgoing young woman, after all—she couldn't resist taking a few moments to be herself. Her life had involved so many pretenses at so many times that sometimes she was left drained and exhausted.

The Dog Star Saloon was the roughest dive in town, not the kind of place decent young women visited. Just now that made it quite appealing to Julia Canton. She headed there with a determined stride, and when she entered the place, there was a noticeable lull in the level of noise as every person in the place looked at her, stunned to see such perfect beauty in a place of such base ugliness.

As she sat down in a corner so as to have a good view of anyone who approached her, she wondered how Mrs. Bewley would react if she knew her dress shop assistant was camping herself out in a low-class saloon as if she were some common cyprian. It didn't much matter: The dress shop job was merely a time-passer, and a means of keeping a few extra coins in her pocket so she could leave her main resources safely untouched in the Hangtree Bank. If she lost the job, so be it.

In the Dog Star, most patrons placed their orders at the bar or merely hollered them across the room at the proprietor and barkeep, Squint McCray. In Julia Canton's case, Squint himself saved her the trouble, walking to her table with a twisted grin on his homely face. "Good evening, miss."

"Good evening to you, sir."

"What can I bring you?"

Julia Canton knew fully well that at a watering trough like this one would have limited offerings . . . mostly cheap whiskey, with gin and house-brewed beer to supplement—but she couldn't forget the image she needed to maintain before the watching public. She smiled up at Squint like an angel and spoke in her sweetest voice. "Might you have any sherry wine, sir?"

Had anyone else asked that question at any other time, Squint would have damned him for a fool and uppity swell. No such treatment for such a lovely as this one, though. And as luck would have it, he actually did have a small supply of quite good blackberry wine given to him by a male cousin who had passed through town a month before. The cousin's wife, recently deceased, had loved the stuff and her husband couldn't stand it, so when she passed on he dumped the remaining wine on good old Cousin Squint, who went on to secretly develop a taste for the wine and often sipped a small glass of it before retiring to bed.

Squint told Julia that while he had no sherry, he could offer her an "excellent blackberry wine" from his own stores. He beamed down at her in anticipation of a grateful thank-you and broad smile, but Julia was disappointed and unable to hide it for a couple of moments. Her plan had been to put on a pretense of "settling" for whiskey in the absence of wine, but Squint's brother-in-law and his cast-off blackberry wine ruined that game for her. Forcing out a smile, she accepted Squint's offered wine with seeming gratitude. Squint strode back to his little office behind the bar to fetch her drink, thinking himself both clever and lucky.

Julia sipped the wine, which was better than she anticipated, and looked at the room around her, mostly using peripheral vision to avoid looking directly back at the many men in the place blatantly staring at her. Sending signals of returned interest could in this kind of setting be not only socially awkward, but downright dangerous. There was already one man creeping around in the shadows at her heels; certainly she did not want an entire parade of such.

Squint had recently persuaded one of the local soiled doves, Petunia Scranton, that she had missed her calling, and should have been what he called a "French dancer." By this he was referring to the three-decades-old dance style known as "can-can." The girl, who hated the life of giving herself to foul and unwashed men who treated her merely as a receptacle, had taken Squint's assessment to heart. When she begged him for the chance to perform the can-can in his saloon to entertain customers, he'd felt obliged to give her the chance. He built a tiny stage in one of the front corners, just big enough to accommodate one person, and hung it about with dark curtains borrowed from the local undertaker's funeral parlor. On her tiny stage, and wearing a flouncing skirt, petticoats, ruffled drawers, and a literally painted-on smile, she'd begun performing her high-kicking dance in her corner and drawing hearty applause, especially in her first days, when her poorly secured and oversized shoes had tended to kick off her feet and hit members of her audience in the face.

The music for her dance was provided by Charlotte Pugh, another local whore who had at some time in girlhood been taught to play three songs on the piano. One of these was a slow waltz, totally lacking the speed and rhythm required by can-can. The other two were old camp meeting hymns, mournful and dirge-like in their original form, but danceable enough when sped up to three times their normal pace. Thus, evening after evening, Petunia Scranton found herself doing the can-can (sometimes, when Squint wasn't watching closely and she could get away with it, without her drawers) to a fast-paced piano rendition of "I Will Arise and Go to Jesus." It made the tiny, lingering bit of "decent girl" left in her feel horribly irreligious, but she figured it was at least better than selling herself to drunks in back alleys.

The music began and the high kicking followed, drawing men to the front where they could get a good look at Squint's "French dancer." Julia thus found herself in the pleasant circumstance of being in a public setting and yet not being stared at by anyone, at least as best she could tell. She took a sip of Squint's blackberry wine and had a moment of authentic, pure enjoyment of her life.

When one was accustomed to the constant sting of probing stares, one longed for privacy with a passion approaching lust. Julia had learned that lesson even before she came of age.

She noticed the photograph of the dead Toleen brother standing on an easel in the corner opposite the little dancing stage, and a chill struck.

"Miz Canton, I believe," said a man's voice from somewhere to the side of her. Startled, she turned her head and saw Sam Heller only a couple of yards away. He'd managed to approach her in utter silence and without any stray movements to pull her eye his way. She knew who he was because he had been pointed out to her one day as he came out of the Hangtree Bank while she was dodging the heat of the sun on a shaded porch nearby. She'd watched his impressive form closely that day, and at this moment, was equally drawn to his handsome and weathered face.

"Mr. Sam Heller, I think?" she said, setting her wineglass on the table and pushing it aside a few inches. Heller possessed a drink as well, whiskey in a shot glass that looked absurdly tiny in his big hand. Julia flicked her eyes toward the empty chair on the other side of the little round table, and Heller moved there, scooted it back with his foot, and sat down. The chair creaked under his weight.

"So you don't mind if I sit?"

"Not at all, Mr. Heller. I'm glad for the company."

"How is it you know me?" he asked her.

"I saw you in town and asked someone who you were. And how do you know me, sir?"

"First off, don't call me no sir or nothing. Nor mister. Just Sam."

"Only if you'll call me Julia." She gave him a smile that would have thawed a man made of pure ice into a spreading puddle.

"To answer your question, I know you because, just now, I don't think there's a soul in Hangtree who don't know who Julia Canton is. You turned the heads and caught the eyes of every man in this county the day you got here."

"Every man in the county, you say? Well, I'm impressed with myself if that's the case."

"Don't get too proud, ma'am. It's a small county."

She laughed and Heller broke into a grin. She thought it a beautiful style and him a handsome man.

"So where's my old compadre Johnny Cross?" Heller asked.

She sipped her wine and shrugged. "I wouldn't

know, nor know why I should be expected to know."

"You been seen with him a good deal these last days, walking beside him in the streets, eating meals with him at the Cattleman."

"An appealing man asks to keep me company or buy me a good beefsteak, and I'm not one to turn that down."

"Julia, I don't know whether you find me appealing or not, but there's something I'd like to ask of you, if Johnny ain't beat me to it already."

"Ask away."

"There's a dance coming up, and if you're the dance-going type, I'd like to ask you to accompany me."

She finished her little glass of wine and studied the dark droplets lingering in the bottom of it. She caught Squint's eye and raised the glass to ask for a refill. He hustled to get the bottle.

"The truth is, no one has asked me already. And yes, Sam, I'd be pleased to go with you. Though I admit to dreading hearing the fiddle music. The man who plays it lives in the same boarding-house and has been practicing a lot where I can hear it. He'll not likely win any fiddling contests."

"Claude does the best he can."

"Why don't I find that encouraging?"

Heller laughed. "I understand. I do. But I got to like Claude. He's a good man."

Squint showed up with the bottle of black-berry wine and refreshed Julia's glass. He was forced to explain to Heller what the blue-black libation was, and how he'd come to have it. Heller turned down an invitation to try some for himself.

Squint returned to the bar and Heller and Julia fell into conversation, getting to know one another, sharing what parts of their backgrounds they felt comfortable with. Heller, who had possessed a strong interest in the southernmost states since knowing many southerners during the war, quizzed her closely about her Georgia childhood. Only when he noticed she seemed to be made uncomfortable by the questions and unable in some cases to answer readily, did he desist.

He tried not to think about it, but something just didn't feel quite right in it all.

"Now, let me ask you some questions," she said. "When I was a little girl, my Sunday school teacher told me that God owns the cattle on a thousand hills. Then I got to Hangtree, Texas, and heard from most around me that, no, it ain't the Lord, it's Sam Heller who owns those cattle. Is that right?"

"If you're counting on cattle on hills, that'd amount to a small herd to own for either man or Lord," Sam said. "Not many hills worthy of the name to be found around here."

"I noticed."

"But if you're talking about longhorns in general, hill cattle or flatland cattle, well, I reckon I do own my share of them, and a few more shares besides."

"Richest man in the region, I'm told."

"Is 'rich' an important thing to you?"

She reached over and laid the flat of her forefinger on the nail of one of his. "Let's say that it doesn't lessen my interest, and in fact might just make it all the stronger."

He smiled and grasped her hand, holding it in his there on the tabletop. She did not pull away, and it pleased him.

"Why do you carry such a strange weapon?" she asked. "I saw it on you one day when you came out of the bank. More of a rifle than a pistol."

"I've found I naturally favor it," he said. "I'm a better shot with it than with a standard pistol, though sometimes, like tonight, I'll switch it out for a Colt if I'm going to be in town and don't want such a showy weapon on me. But I prefer the mule-leg. Other folks have trouble with mule-leg guns, but me, it's like a natural extension of my arm. I just think of what I want to hit, raise, and fire, and nine times out of ten I've hit what I wanted."

"Sounds like you might be a very dangerous man," Julia said.

Heller shook his head. "I wouldn't say that. I'm no danger at all to those who give me no cause to be such to them. In fact, in the case of good, honest people, I'm a protector, not a danger."

"Even if the people are good, honest rebs? I've been told you were a Yankee during the war, and that a lot of folks here call you a carpetbagger."

"People 'call' a lot of things. Most ain't worth listening to. Here's the way I look at it: War's over. Time to get on with the peace, and the coming back together. The dividing up just got a lot of folks killed."

She grew thoughtful and looked past him, up toward the front of the saloon. She stared at the ugly, gray image of the dead Toleen brother with his empty eye sockets.

"It's hard to put the past behind, though," she said. "Hard to forget what you've been through. Where you came from, and who you came from."

"You're a philosopher, good lady."

She smiled. "And you, sir, are a fine specimen of a man."

"Better specimen than Johnny Cross?"

"Better than anybody I can think of. Can you walk me back to my boardinghouse?"

"I can."

She drained off the last of her blackberry wine and slipped her arm into the crook of his. As they walked out of the Dog Star, she paused and glanced at the Toleen image.

"Cal," she said.

"Beg pardon?"

"Cal. That's Cal Toleen there."

"Is that right? As I was hearing things, nobody was sure which one of the twins this one was."

"It's Cal."

"Begging pardon again, but how would you know?"

She was discomfited by the question, but shrugged past it and said merely, "You know what you know."

Sam looked at the face of the man he had tied to the back of Otto Perkins's wagon to drag into town. "Evening, Cal," he said, and led the prettiest woman in Texas out the door of the Dog Star into the Hangtree dark.

CHAPTER THIRTEEN

Julia slept restlessly that night, not as the result of blackberry wine or feet sore from a long meandering walk around the dark town with Sam Heller. What kept stirring her back to wakefulness was a sense of not being truly alone, a feeling that someone was out there, in the dark beyond the boardinghouse walls. Maybe watching, maybe just pacing about. But out there because of her.

She dreamed during her sporadic periods of sleeping, the dreams being a combination of memories from childhood and imaginations about the person she was convinced was out there. She dreamed it was Sam Heller, and Johnny Cross. That it was that strange picture-taking fellow whose shop Johnny had led her into that day he was trying to find a man who had a knife for sale. She dreamed it was Timothy Holt out there, angry and heartbroken and suddenly no longer the gentle, boyish fellow who reminded her so much of her late brother. Then in the dream he changed all at once to Cal Toleen, the dead outlaw in the picture back at the saloon, and he was walking around out there with his skin gray and crumbling, and his eyes missing.

That mental vision woke her up and she sat up slowly in her bed, looking at the open second-floor window on the north wall of her room and listening to the night outside. "Papa?" she said, nonsensically, because she knew that if anyone was really out there at all, it was not and could not be her father. But the feeling was strong. "Papa? Is that you?"

There was a reply. No dream, it seemed. A real voice, one she did not know, rising up from below the window in a whisper just loud enough for her to hear. It chilled her as it said, "Della Rose? Della Rose, dear girl, it's time to come home."

She collapsed back into the bed and covered her face with her arms, hardly allowing herself even to breathe. She heard footsteps outside, or thought she did, though at some level of her mind she knew it was just a dream. No one would be out there, not really.

"Come on soon, Della Rose. Everyone is waiting for you at home. Come on."

She did not know the voice. So why did she dream it? If her fancies were going to tell her that was her father out there, why did the man not have her father's voice? And why did he call her

Della Rose? That was not her. Not anymore. Della Rose belonged to a past best forgotten by all. Especially by Julia Canton.

She remembered then the man she'd seen in town, seemingly watching her from the other side of the street outside the dress shop. And she'd seen him other places as well. Maybe it was his voice she'd heard, if she'd actually heard one at all.

But he was a stranger. How did he know about Della Rose? And what did he know?

Closing her eyes tightly, she closed out the room and the night and with a pillow tried also to close out any voice that rose from inside herself, or from outside her window.

She looked for footprints outside the boardinghouse the next morning, and found them, but they meant nothing and she knew it. People walked in the dirt alley behind the boardinghouse all the time. It was a favorite shortcut toward a busy farrier's shop. Footprints were to be expected.

In the rising daylight, some of her fear of the prior night seemed rather silly. Clearly she'd slept badly and been disturbed by dreams, and in dreams people saw and heard all kinds of things that weren't really happening. She knew it now and she'd known it in the night while she lay trembling under her covers, afraid to peep out at her window because she feared that framed in it she'd see the face of the stranger who had been watching her lately, or that of the disturbing photographer who had taken the photograph of Cal Toleen and who seemed familiar to her for reasons she could not explicate, or maybe the face of her father, looking for her to tell her to come home, using a voice not his own.

She swore softly and stamped her foot in the dirt. If it would have helped, she might have slapped her own face, trying to knock some sense and reality back into her head. She looked up at the sky, not to pray, but to see clouds and blue and birds flying overhead . . . real things, things that were material and solid and part of the world that had nothing to do with phantom voices and the footfalls of people outside who were not really there.

Drawing in a deep breath, she reminded herself that she was not in this ugly little town for no reason. There was a purpose, and at the moment she'd taken an important step in the direction of fulfilling it. She'd met Sam Heller and drawn him to her, using her charm and her beauty and the simple fact that she was cunning and smart and not one to let herself be thrown off her task by nervousness or boredom or ridiculous dreams.

"Once you set yourself a task, stay on it until it is done," she said to herself, softly but aloud. Her father had told her that. "Stay on it even if the Lord above and devil below put theirselves in common bond against you to stop you. Keep on doing and going and doing. Till it's done."

She drew in long, deep breaths, and caught the whiff of frying bacon from her landlady's kitchen. Fiddling Claude Farley and his wife, Hilda, and all the other dullards who shared the boardinghouse with Julia would be gathering around the big table to gnaw on thick slices of bacon, fried hard, and mounds of scrambled eggs. Runny. And biscuits baked into bricks.

The food was poor, the company worse, but hunger was hunger and Julia needed to eat. She shook off the last of her tension from the difficult night before and went through the mudroom door into the boardinghouse, prepared to smile and be cordial and shallow and get through the meal so she could start her day.

"I heard some man talking out behind the house last night," said Hilda Farley around a mouthful of biscuit. "Couldn't make out what he was saying, for it was just like a loud whisper, but there was somebody."

"You dreamed it, Hildy, I told you that," said Claude.

"I heard it, not dreamed it. Know it for a fact."

"Which calls upon us to do what in response?" Claude said. "Hmm? Hmm?"

"Nothing, husband. Nothing."

"No point in bringing it up at all, then, was there?" Claude said. "Somebody pass me the bacon plate."

* * *

Sweeping was sweeping, Timothy Holt supposed, but even so, sweeping in Otto Perkins's photography shop and studio felt entirely different and new in comparison to sweeping at the Emporium. Timothy had no problems on the boardwalk outside, which was merely a smaller version of the same kind that was at the Lockhart Emporium, but inside Timothy was forever bumping into things: a metal bracket that was designed to help hold motionless the heads of people seated in a chair to be photographed, a big, umbrella-like reflector used to direct and intensify light, and various cases of things Timothy could not attach any explanation to at all. He felt clumsy and stupid, bumping into everything he got near to, and hoped his new employer would not fire him on his very first day.

He learned quickly that Perkins was not a natural-born shopkeeper. He'd turned his rolling photographic business into a fixed one mostly by merely moving items from his wagon into this rented space, but he'd left it all in such haphazard state that it appeared he was trying to keep things ready to move back onto the wagon as fast as he'd moved them off.

When Timothy had gotten the floors as clean as he could make them, he became distracted by the big volumes of old photographs made over the years and miles by Otto Perkins. Without really being able to express it to himself in words, he was fascinated with the concept that pieces of people's lives were frozen and trapped in those volumes, images of them as they were at a moment they were thinking a particular thought, experiencing a specific feeling, looking at something outside the range of the photograph that now held them. Had fate and development been kinder to him, Timothy Holt might have been a skilled abstract thinker.

Otto Perkins busied around the place, but for the most part left Timothy to his sweeping. He was glad to have another person about the place, even one who offered only limited options for conversation. As a traveling man most of the time, Perkins was accustomed to being often alone and usually didn't mind it. But humans were made for company, not loneliness.

Then, watching Timothy pause in his sweeping and stare again at the bound volumes of old photographs, Perkins remembered what he told Timothy before. There was something he wanted to show him, to see if Timothy saw it the same way he did. He called the young man over.

"Timothy, I'm going to show you a particular old photograph I took twelve years ago in eastern Texas. It's a picture of a particular old outlaw and his people, his family. I have taken many pictures of outlaws, you know, and plan to put them out as a collection someday. Do you understand what I mean by that?"

"Yes, sir," Timothy muttered.

"Come on." He led Timothy to a big desk that came with his rented office space. Trudging to the storage shelf where he kept the bound volumes, he got the one he wanted and brought it to the desk. Full of tintypes, it was heavy and went down onto the desktop with a loud thud. He opened it and began turning over image after image, most of them unremarkable, significant only because of the infamy of some of those pictured.

"And here we are," Perkins said at last, laying the volume wide at a particular photograph showing a line of people ranging from children through elderly individuals. They were lined up side by side, some seated in the foreground, others standing behind or beside them, all looking somber and rigid. In the center of the photograph, standing taller than any of the others, was the figure of a middle-aged man with harshly glaring eyes, the scars of old burns marring the skin on one side of his face, and on that same side, partially hidden by his hair, a black nub where an ear should be. As he looked over the faces in the picture, Timothy's eye was drawn always back to the grim, scary face of the tall man.

"You took this picture, Mr. Otto?"

"I did. Under the hire of that man right there." Perkins pointed at the image of the tall man. "He wanted a picture of himself with his family, because he seldom got to be with them. You know who that is, Timothy?"

"No, sir, no. But I don't think I much like him. He has a mean look to him."

"And a mean spirit inside of him. A regular demon of a spirit. He was as hard and cruel as he looks, Timothy. That man is the worst outlaw and criminal I've ever photographed. Have you heard of Black Ear Skinner?"

Timothy mouthed the name, then shoved his face down to look more closely at the tall man's face. "Is that him? Is that Black Ear Skinner?"

"That's him, Timothy. The man himself. That woman beside him, with the pretty face and that sweet look, that's his wife, Belle. Every bit as kindly looking as her husband was vicious. How such a gentle woman wound up married to such a wicked man is a mystery to me. But that pair isn't the most interesting thing in this picture, Timothy. Look at the ones standing beside them. Their children."

Timothy looked closely. There was a boy, standing closely beside his mother, his hand up and clinging to hers. Something in the boy's look seemed unusual, absent. Beside the boy was a tall girl, light-haired and with a face like her father's, without the wickedness. And beside her, a second girl, dark-haired and younger, and not nearly as tall as her gangly sister. Timothy barely glanced at the second girl at first, then suddenly locked in on her face. She appeared to be perhaps ten years old, maybe eleven . . . and though Timothy knew no children of that age just now, he knew he'd conversed with this girl very recently.

It hit him: It was Julia Canton. A younger version of her, yes, but obviously Julia Canton.

"Is that . . . is she . . ."

"Yes," said Perkins. "I knew when I saw our

lovely Miss Canton that I recognized her from somewhere. It just took me a little time to remember, then to study that picture long enough to be sure. It has been years, after all."

"But why is Miss Julia with an outlaw's family?"

"Because she's part of it, Timothy. She isn't who she told us she was. Julia Canton isn't Julia Canton. Her name is Skinner. According to my old notes I made to go with this group of photographs, her name is Della. Della Rose Skinner. Daughter of the infamous Black Ear Skinner himself."

CHAPTER FOURTEEN

A few miles southwest of the town of Hangtree, the remnants of what might have become a town, but for an act of God, broke the monotony of the flatlands. Resurrection Gulch had a history as strange as it was short. Created at the close of the war, the little settlement had been formed and populated by an idealistic band of Confederates and Confederate sympathizers from Arkansas who had centered their life around a politicized church led by a radical minister. That minister claimed divinely granted knowledge that the Confederacy would be resurrected in Texas and be centered in their tiny, barren little flatland farrago. This time, the preacher wildly declared, the Confederacy would thrive rather than fail, and be blessed by the hand of God himself, becoming grander and greater than the United States. Thus it had been revealed and thus it would be.

The starry-eyed pioneers of Resurrection had

plenty of faith but little in the way of finances and the kinds of life experience and skills that might have helped them put down sustaining roots in the Texas soil. None knew how to manage livestock or pursue the limited kind of agriculture appropriate to a dry, sun-baked region. Most lacked skill in working with tools and the kinds of building materials available in the Pecos country. There appeared to be little hope the utopian community would survive, and indeed it did not. The collapse of the little society presaged a far more literal collapse brought on by a tornado that swept past Hangtree but slammed Resurrection hard, leaving little standing but a few isolated walls that stood out rather starkly on the largely empty landscape.

No truly complete building remained at Resurrection Gulch, though the church building was mostly intact. No congregations gathered there now, however, the building being a haven for birds and wildlife, and the occasional traveler who took a night's shelter beneath what remained of the roof.

Companion to the abandoned community was an equally abandoned ranch, similarly damaged by the same tornado and now just an available shelter for man and beast fortunate enough to find it at just the right moment.

Johnny Cross sat astride his horse on a low, broad rise of land and looked down on Resurrection Gulch, knowing he was facing a conversation, soon, with Sam Heller. He knew enough of

Heller's business to see that there were things happening in and around this little ghost community that Heller needed to know about. Otherwise, Cross suspected, Heller stood to lose much he had worked hard to gain and preserve.

Cross was seeing clear signs of occupancy where there should be vacancy, activity where there should be stillness. It was far from clear, however, exactly what was going on. The presence of huge rope corrals out across formerly abandoned ranch lands, and clear evidence that someone was quietly rounding up cattle and herding them together regardless of brand and ownership, raised disturbing questions Johnny Cross could not answer.

He watched awhile longer, then turned his horse and began the ride back to Hangtree.

Otto Perkins was pleased with his new employee. Timothy Holt, though "feeble-minded," was more capable than Perkins had anticipated he would be. His duties expanded beyond mere sweeping to general maintenance of the weakly constructed building. Upon learning that Timothy had some skills in carpentry, basic and unrefined but skills nonetheless, Perkins sent him poking all around his building, inside and out, with hammer and nails to repair damaged areas and strengthen weak ones, of which there were plenty. The building had been damaged in high

winds that had spun off the tornado that had
destroyed the settlement of Resurrection Gulch.

Perkins had taken his growing trust of Timothy
a step further on this particular day. Thinking increasingly of lengthening his stay in Hangtree
and putting the nomadic photographer life behind
him for a year or two, Perkins had developed a
vision of how his rented building might be im-
proved internally to increase its appeal to potential customers. He'd set up a lunch meeting with
the owner of the building to put forth his ideas
and propose that Timothy Holt be used to do
much of the work, which would all be simple: new
shelving, a space divider or two, nothing costly or
hard to accomplish.

Thus it was that Perkins left Timothy to man
the shop alone for the first time while he kept his
lunch meeting. Timothy was merely to keep up
his usual maintenance work and politely instruct
any customers who might come in to return in
the afternoon, when Perkins would be back.

Timothy was sweeping the floor beneath the
front window when he looked up to see Johnny
Cross riding in, fresh from his observation of the
odd activity going on at the Resurrection Gulch
ghost town. On Timothy's mind was the information he'd learned from Perkins about Julia
Canton—Timothy still thought of her by that
name even though he now knew better—and he
decided that Johnny Cross needed to know it as
well. Though he was sure Perkins would not
favor him sharing what had been told to him,

Timothy went to the door and called to Johnny Cross, waving for him to ride over.

"What's going on, Timothy?"

"There's something I need to show you, Mr. Johnny."

"Are you all right?"

"I'm fine. I just know something you'll want to know, too."

Wondering if he were a fool to be snapping at bait thrown out by a simpleton, Johnny Cross even so dismounted and tied his horse off to the porch rail. Timothy led him inside.

"What is it, then?"

"Come back here for a minute . . . I got a picture you need to look at. There's somebody in it who you know."

Puzzled and sure he was wasting his time on something trivial, Cross went along anyway, and followed Timothy back into the room where Perkins stored the big volumes that held his life's work.

"You're going to be surprised," Timothy said in a gleeful tone.

"I don't always like surprises, Tim."

"This may be one of them you don't like, Mr. Johnny. But you'll sure be interested in it!"

And he was. Timothy had to go three times through his version of the narrative that Perkins had given him to manage to convey it accurately to Johnny Cross. At first Cross was inclined to put it all down as an error of some sort, but each time his eye went back to the image of the young girl's face in the lineup of Black Ear Skinner's family, he knew it was Julia Pepperday Canton he was seeing. There was simply no mistaking it: this was Julia as a younger girl, just as stunning then as she was these years later.

Except she wasn't really Julia Canton. Clearly Julia Canton, daughter of a Georgia preacher and good churchgoing young lady, was a fiction. A covering falsehood used by the daughter of an infamous late outlaw to hide herself as if under a cloak.

But why here? Black Ear Skinner had no specific ties to Hangtree or its environs that Johnny Cross knew of. So why would his daughter hide her identity and come here, of all places?

And why, at the same time, would old criminal associates of Black Ear himself begin appearing in the vicinity, robbing Sunday morning church folk, getting themselves shot dead on the roadside, or gunned down in front of the Lockhart Emporium for the sake of so trivial a bit of fun as mocking a half-wit?

Having just been disturbed by unexpected activity out at what was essentially a ghost town, and now by this unexpected revelation about a beautiful young lady he had thought he knew, Johnny Cross had the strongest notion that something odd indeed was going on in Hangtree County. He just had no idea what it was.

"Timothy, do me a favor," he said.

"Anything, Mr. Johnny."

"Let's just keep this private for now, can we?

Don't tell anybody else what you've just told me, or show anybody else this picture here."

"I . . . well, all right. Truth is, Mr. Otto probably wouldn't have wanted me even to show it to you."

"Maybe not. But I'm glad you did. There's something coming into shape around this town that seems to tie back to Black Ear Skinner. And that, my friend, is not likely to prove out to be good news. Nothing involving Skinner can be anything but bad news."

"That makes me feel sad, Mr. Johnny. I don't like bad news."

"Neither do I. Now, Timothy, you put all this back like it was so that Perkins don't have any notion it's been disturbed. I'm going to get out of here before he gets back and finds me here."

"You don't want me to tell him I showed you this, then?"

"No. No. Like I said, let's just keep this private for now. I need to try to figure out just what's going on. By the way, I know you are fond of her, and I'm regretful you had to see her exposed as a falsity."

"It don't matter now, Mr. Johnny. I don't like her no more. I . . . I . . . you'll think me a fool for this, but I tried to get her to go to the dance with me. Got her a flower and everything. She told me she didn't want to go with me."

"Well, she ain't going with me, either, Tim. I guess we both lost out, huh?"

"I reckon." Timothy's eyes were gazing out

through the open door into the room where they were, and out the front window of the store. "Hey, I think that's Jimbo Hale out there across the street. You still wanting to buy that knife off him?"

"I sure am, Timothy. Thanks for spotting him. I'll go out and collar him right now while I got the chance. You get this all put back like it was before we came in here, you hear?"

"I sure do, Mr. Johnny. I hope Jimbo ain't sold that knife yet."

"I heard tell he was still trying to sell it as recent as yesterday," Cross replied. "He's asking too much for it, though. I'll see if I can't talk him down on it a little."

Timothy nodded and began putting back in place the items they had disturbed. By the time Otto Perkins got back to his shop and studio, grinning privately from a successful meeting with his landlord, Timothy was repairing loose trim on a side window, the shop was in good order, and Johnny Cross had, ten minutes before, rode off on his horse, the proud possessor of a new knife.

CHAPTER FIFTEEN

"Julia? Can you come back here a moment?"

Startled by the call from Mrs. Bewley, Julia Canton moved too quickly and overturned a display of stacked thimbles she had just finished on the flat display area of the front window—no easily achieved task. She swore softly beneath her breath, hoped Mrs. Bewley hadn't heard it, and breezed back to the storeroom.

"Yes, Mrs. Bewley?"

"Julia, dear, I've got something for you. You've done so well here at the store, and increased our business so much, that you've earned a little something extra. And here it is."

Mrs. Bewley reached behind a bolt of cloth that had been put aside because insects had damaged it, and pulled out a beautiful lavender dress. She held it up proudly.

"It's beautiful, Mrs. Bewley. Absolutely beautiful!"

"It's yours, Julia, if you'll have it. I've had this

cloth laid back in store for some special use for a long time now, waiting for a special time I could use it. Having you join me here has given me reason to bring it out and sew you this dress. I hope so much that it fits you well . . . I think it will, because I've had so much experience in measuring for dresses that I've gotten to where I can do it just from looking, and almost always be right down to the inch. My hope is you'll like it well enough to wear it to the dance this week. I'm assuming you'll have many men ask you to go."

"Oh, Mrs. Bewley . . . may I try it on now? I love it! Adore it! You are so very kind, so kind, to do this for me!"

"Certainly. Would you like me to help you into it?"

"I can do it alone. I'll come out and let you see it, though. And yes, I am going to the dance. Sam Heller invited me."

"Oh!" Mrs. Bewley's brows went up in a knowing and pleased expression. "Richest man in Hangtree, that one! Well done, dear!"

The dress fit perfectly, and its color brought out all that was best in the flawless young woman. She paraded it proudly before Mrs. Bewley, authentically grateful to the older woman for her gift, and caught herself wondering what Sam Heller would have to say when he saw her so beautifully garbed.

She'd knock his eyes out, and knew it. And the

eyes of every other man at that dance. Every man would wish she was with him, and every other female there, young and old, would envy her for the ease with which she would steal the show.

She wouldn't even have to try. Julia Pepperday Canton had always stolen the show, wherever she was and whomever she was with. As had Della Rose Skinner before her, the identity she had left behind and to which she would soon return, if all went according to plan.

Della Rose Skinner had been fortunate enough to inherit the beauty of her mother, and somehow to build on it and render it perfect. How a man as physically unappealing as Curry "Black Ear" Skinner had managed to snare such a lovely woman as Belle Pepperday was a mystery to all, including Curry himself. That Rose had aligned herself with a man of such amoral criminality and cruelty was even more astonishing. Rose had been the daughter of a Georgia preacher of stern and uncompromising moral standards, determined his daughter would marry no man who did not share his principles. That it was the old preacher himself who had first introduced youthful Curry Skinner to Della was one of life's ironies. Of course, at that time Curry Skinner had been presenting himself to the world as a reverend himself, preaching some excellent sermons at camp meetings and church gatherings across the South. The outlaw persona of the man had yet to become known.

The kin of Black Ear Skinner always said that goodness showed itself only in three areas of the man's life. One was the gentle care he provided for his wife when a stroke she suffered during the birth of their son, Jimmy, left her in a coma destined to become her perpetual state of existence. Black Ear made sure his wife had the best doctors, nurses, and housekeepers to see that her world was as safe and pleasant as it could be, though the comatose Rose knew nothing of any of it. The second was in the way Black Ear protected and supported his only son, despite the fact that it was in that son's birth that his wife suffered her life-changing affliction. Jimmy suffered in the difficult birth, and was left with a weak heart and slowed mental growth. Never to view the world with anything beyond a three-year-old's level of maturity, Jimmy was destined to life as a "half-wit," as many people of the time called such as he. No one dared label him so in Black Ear's presence, however: Black Ear, on one of the rare occasions he dared to be in his own home despite imminent danger of arrest, once shot a dinner guest through the forehead after the man complained of "that stupid half-wit" knocking over his drink at the table. The bullet went through the unwise man's forehead and blew blood and matter all over the wall behind the dinner table. Black Ear forbade anyone thereafter from replacing the splattered wallpaper, saying he found the ragged stain of blackened crimson "pretty."

The third and final aspect of life in which Black Ear exhibited anything approaching goodness was in the way he treated his only daughter,

Della Rose (who in later years would borrow liberally from her mother's life story and maiden name in forging her persona of Julia Pepperday Canton, including her mentally slow brother). Having been impoverished in childhood, Black Ear was determined his girl would have what she needed in life and never go hungry or raggedly clothed. An astonishing story was often repeated among Black Ear's kin, quoting him as saying he sometimes prayed to God in thanks that his daughter had been blessed with extraordinary beauty, because it would make her life's journey easier. The amazing thing about it was the idea of Black Ear Skinner saying any kind of prayer beyond the contrived and false ones he'd performed back in his days as a fraudulent preacher.

Black Ear's love for Della Rose was most clearly shown, it was said in the family, by the way he arranged for an expensive and high-quality education for her. He sent her off to a prestigious academy in the East, where she thrived and learned to present herself before the world to her own greatest advantage. She completed her education with the highest grades and honors, though under a fictional name and biography. Black Ear was aware of his daughter's vulnerability to unscrupulous manhunters who might threaten her safety to gain leverage over one of the nation's most wanted and hated outlaws. Della's teachers and fellow students never knew their exemplary and amazingly beautiful fellow scholar, Julia Canton, was the daughter of an infamous and despised outlaw.

Della had found it easy to live under a false identity. It solved many problems simply by not bringing them up in the first place. There was never need to apologize for being the daughter of a minister. She fit in with normal society, and once people "knew" her good-girl background, expectations for her were that she would be a young woman of good repute and high moral code. So it was easy to brush off the many men who were lured by her beauty for lustful reasons.

Her professions of being a righteous girl were as false as her name. Julia Pepperday Canton might have been the well-behaved daughter of a southern preaher, but Della Rose Skinner had been born to a man of sin and carried his blood in her veins. It fueled an interest in the same things that had driven her father: greed, the desire for fast and unfettered fulfillment of impulses and wishes, and the prospect that perhaps one really could reap something other than what was sown.

It hadn't turned out that way for Black Ear, of course. He'd lived by the gun and died the same way. Died in commission of a robbery, and the jolt of losing her father and seeing his gang of gunhawks scatter for their own safety, like disturbed quail, had changed something inside of Della Rose. Any battle between the Julia side of her and the Della side had instantly tilted, and Della Rose had found herself beginning to dream of claiming her family legacy in a way no one would anticipate . . . she would drape her father's fallen mantle over her own shoulders and find a way to bring the Black Ear gang back together in a way that would do true honor to the memory of his name and legacy.

At the beginning she'd tried to make herself believe that the best way to honor her father would be to devote herself wholeheartedly to the care of her incapacited mother. He'd cared about her so deeply, and surely it would have pleased him to know that someone was stepping in who would care as well.

So Della had tried. She'd sat beside her mother, reading aloud to her though there was no indication the woman could hear. She sang songs her mother had loved before her apoplexy and washed her brow with damp, cool cloths when the weather was hot. As much as she loved Rose Skinner, though, she could not escape the fact she was really doing her no good. Della was quite sure her mother had no notion even of her own existence, much less who she was and who it was who cared for her.

Della couldn't go on with it. Her mother's needs were being met by paid nurses and domestics (most of them not knowing their pay came from the proceeds of crime), and Della was restless and unhappy, and feeling that her father was being forgotten. For Della that was intolerable. To her, if to no one else, Black Ear Skinner had been a great and memorable man.

So she decided to find a way to take his place. Using fact-finding research skills that had made her a leading student at her prestigious academy for young ladies, she began contriving a criminal plan her father would have been proud to pursue, and to look for a place it could be done. She had some advantages her late father would not have possessed had he been the one putting the plan into motion. She was female and beautiful, cultured and educated, and very cunning. And she would be leading a gang that no one believed existed any longer, not since the death of Black Ear effectively cut off their head.

The research was done, the plan formalized. Della got in contact with the members of the Black Ear gang whom her father had deemed the most trustworthy, and recruited them to begin the process of reconstructing the old gang, though not in full. Della Rose's version of the Black Ears would be made up only of the best of their number, men who could be counted on and who would have been the ones her father would have chosen. That, at least, was her goal. Della would later come to realize that some from the older and lesser ranks of the gang had caught wind that something was in the works, and managed to find their way into the fringes of it as uninvited and unwanted hangers-on. One of them, a true old-timer as Black Ears went, had been relieved of his teeth by Della herself in the Hangtree Church when the fool tried to rob the congregants and also threatened to blunderingly expose her identity. Another had gotten himself killed by Sam Heller's mule-leg rifle in front of the Lockhart Emporium.

Before all that happened, though, the plan was put in place. Some of the process seemed downright providential, or at least serendipitous. She explored the possibility of hiring the famed Pinkerton detective organization to help her gather a list of names of wealthy Texas men who might be good prospects for her scheme (she told the Pinkertons nothing of what her real motives were, nor what her real identity was). In the process of talking to her Pinkerton contact, she used her well-practiced charm and managed to learn of a former wartime Pinkerton named Sam Heller who was reportedly making quite a pile of wealth for himself down below the Staked Plains in an unknown little smattering of buildings known as the town of Hangtree. As remote and incognito a place as one could find, it seemed an ideal locale at which to stage an audacious scheme such as Della Rose wished to put into motion. And a possible shape for that scheme fell into place when Della learned that Sam Heller, who had worked for the Pinkertons during the war, was a man who reportedly had nearly $100,000 banked in the little town, more hidden at some unidentified location in the area, and uncounted numbers of longhorn cattle on the plains near Hangtree and Fort Pardee, the nearest military outpost in the region. "So many cattle you could likely trample the town into the earth if you ran enough of them through it at one time," the Pinkerton man said to the lady who had introduced herself as Julia Pepperday Canton and then proceeded to turn him into a babbling fount of information and rumors despite all prior training to give only minimal and verified facts in any situation other than the briefing of Pinkerton superiors.

Della Rose Skinner never hired the Pinkertons, but she did hire a drifter with some police experience to make the journey to Hangtree and find out more about Sam Heller. He'd done his job, and Della Rose knew from his information just who it was who would be first to feel the touch of the revived Black Ear gang. It would be the very man who was to accompany her to the town dance on the coming Friday evening.

And Heller's own longhorns would help clean Heller out.

She hoped her father would have been proud.

CHAPTER SIXTEEN

Early the next morning, as Sam Heller headed toward a steak-and-egg breakfast at the Cattleman, he passed a smokehouse that served the household of an administrator at the Hangtree Bank, one Arvil Caldwell, a man well-known to Heller. It was Caldwell who had helped Heller establish his multiple accounts at the bank, and who served as the unofficial designated guardian of Heller's extensive holdings in gold, silver, and cash in the bank's big vault.

Heller had often chanced to meet Caldwell coming out of his house as Heller headed for breakfast, so he prepared to say his hello should today prove to be one of those days. And it did. The door opened and Caldwell, face ruddy from a fresh morning shave and scrub, came out and grinned at Heller.

"Good morning, Sam! Looks to be a lovely day coming on!"

"Going to be hot, I'd say. You had breakfast?"

"Not yet, no."

"Come on then. I'm buying."

"Well! My lucky day, then!" The smiling man tripped lightly down his porch steps to join Heller. As he did so, his seven-year-old daughter, Angeline, came to the door, bearing a new doll he'd given her for her birthday a week earlier, and gave him a chirpy "Have a good day, Daddy!" He waved back at the girl and told her he hoped the same for her.

"You're a fortunate man, you know it?" Heller said as they walked in the direction of the big hotel that hosted the finest eatery in town. "Pretty wife, good family, nice home, solid work."

"Oh, I know it, Sam. I take not a bit of it for granted. I've been blessed beyond all measure, and don't deserve half of it."

"You take good care of your own, and that counts for a lot. You deserve your blessings more than you realize, Arvil."

"Thank you, Sam." Caldwell paused, then said, "From what I hear, you have some blessings of your own just now. Going to take that lovely new lady down at Myrtle's dress shop to the dance, I'm told."

"Who's been talking about me?"

"The lady herself, Miss Canton. She's been in the bank a good deal lately, making small deposits and every now and then a withdrawal. Half the time she doesn't seem to have all that good a reason to be there. She had one of the tellers give her a tour of the building a couple of days ago. Said she just likes banks and thought our vault door looked 'artistic.' Got a pretty emblem painted on it, you know."

"Yep. I've seen it aplenty. 'Likes banks,' huh? Odd thing to say."

"I thought the same, but I'm not trying to mock her when I tell you that. I hear she is a woman of good reputation."

"We know she goes to church, anyway," Heller said. "Knocked the teeth out of an outlaw's mouth not long ago, right there in the service."

"I know. I was there and I saw it. And heard what the man said to her before she did it, too. Looked right at her and said, 'It's you.'"

"Like he knowed her?"

"Sounded that way to me."

Heller strode along for a bit without saying anything, but he seemed to be thinking hard, and Caldwell noticed.

"Everything all right, Sam?"

"Fine, fine. Will be, anyhow, when I have some grub in my belly." They walked in and sat down at Sam's usual table. "Like she knowed him, huh?"

Caldwell realized the conversation had just turned back to the bit of offering plate violence that had happened that Sunday morning in the Hangtree Church. "Well, I guess really it was more like he knew her than the other way around."

"Troubles me, somehow. That fellow, I'm told, proved out to be an outlaw. No big fish, I don't think, but still an outlaw. Tied in sometime in the past with Black Ear Skinner himself."

Caldwell, a diplomat and appeaser by nature, said, "Think about it, Sam. A woman that beautiful is going to tend to be remembered a good while by any man who sees her. A face and a pair of . . . let me just say, a face and *form* like that tends to lodge itself in a man's mind. Most likely the old fellow had just seen her somewhere before. Maybe just out on the street. Or maybe he rode in on the same stagecoach she did. That might have been the only 'knowing' of each other that was involved."

"Probably so. Hope so."

The waiter appeared in his black vest and matching armbands over a crisp white shirt. "Steak and eggs, Sam?"

"Yep. Same for you, Arvil?"

"Sounds just right."

Coffee was served and they settled in to talk and await their food. "Likes banks," Sam muttered in a distracted manner. "Never heard of somebody who just 'likes banks.'"

"Don't worry so much, Sam. She ain't loco, she's fine. And if she ain't, she's pretty enough to make up for it."

"That's the truth. Just something, though . . . can't quite figure it out. Just something that don't feel right."

"Well, the main thing is, you've got yourself a mighty fine partner to kick up your heels with Friday night."

"No denying."

"Sam, when am I ever going to persuade you

to trust the bank for all your money? Everybody in town says Sam Heller has at least a third of his money hid out somewhere, stashed away, because he figures banks can be robbed."

"That's what they say, is it?"

"You know it is. What I want to know is, is that true?"

"Could be."

"Wherever you've got it—and you should know that folks are guessing about that all the time—I can assure you it would be safer in our vault with the rest of your cash."

"So you tell me. Put all my eggs in one basket and I'll have no worries. Not sure I go along with that."

The arrival of the food ended most of the conversation. Heller paid for the meals when they were done and said his farewell to Caldwell, who headed toward the bank.

. . . And there she was. Julia Canton was on the far side of the street from the bank and looking closely at it. Caldwell stopped where he was and watched her, thinking about the worries Heller had expressed and wondering if there was indeed anything worthy of concern over her odd interest in this particular bank. A bank where, coincidentally or not, a big part of the cash on deposit had been put there by Sam Heller.

The metallic flash passed what seemed mere inches in front of Sam Heller's eyes, close enough to make him start and reflexively reach for his mule-leg sidearm. The hard thunking sound beside him verified what he'd thought: the thing that had flashed by in front of him was a thrown knife, and it was lodged firmly into the wall of the feed store wall beside him.

Heller's weapon was up and ready to fire before he even noticed that the man who'd thrown the knife was Johnny Cross, and Cross was grinning like a cat. "Morning, Sam."

"Johnny, I nigh kilt you."

Cross shook his head. "Seems to me it was me who nigh kilt you. Another five inches to the right and I'd at least have sliced off your nose. A little farther right and that blade would be buried in your temple."

Heller put the mule-leg back into its custom holster and looked at the blade lodged in the plank siding. "Nice knife. Is that the one Jimbo Hale has been trying to sell?"

"That's it. And I'm the one who got it. Good throwing knives, them Arkansas toothpicks are. Got the right balance for it, that one there even better than most."

"Sorry you decided to try to kill me this morning, Johnny."

"If I'd been trying to kill you, we wouldn't be having this conversation right now."

Heller reached up and pulled the knife from the wall. He handed it to Cross. "Your blade, sir."

"Truth is, Sam, I come looking for you. Not

just to show off my new toothpick, either. Couple of things you need to know about."

"Hell, Johnny, you're sounding almost serious just now."

"Maybe it is serious. Or maybe it ain't. I don't know, but I figure the best is just to tell you."

"Speak on, then."

"I was out near Resurrection Gulch yesterday, and there's some odd things going on there-abouts."

Sam looked more startled than he would have intended.

"What do you mean?"

"You got men hired to round up cattle out there?"

"Not at the moment."

"Well, somebody's doing just that. Rope corrals strung up everywhere, and all kinds of cattle. Quite a big herd being put together, and even though I wasn't close enough to see brands, some of them got to be yours."

"Yeah. Could you tell who it was? Recognize anybody?"

"Sure couldn't. But something smelled mighty bad in the whole situation, and I ain't just talking cow pies."

"That kind of worries me, and I won't deny it."

"There's something else, too. Something I learned down at that picture-taking shop. Four-eyes Perkins's place."

"Huh?"

"Something about the lady you're taking to the dance, as I hear it."

Heller paused, frowned, then broke into a knowing smile. "All right, Cross. Now I see it! You were prancing around town with Julia Canton, and all at once you hear she's going to the dance-party with me . . . and you get all green over it. So you decide to tell me my cattle are all getting rustled and all such as that, trying to get me worried and fretful. You're jealous and wishing you'd got around to asking her instead of letting the better man beat you to it."

"'Better man'? Who the hell might *that* be?"

"The one who's stepping out with Julia Canton to that dance, that's who!"

Cross's temper got away from him. He was not one to be made fun of, especially by Sam Heller. Anger overcame judgment. "Her name ain't Julia Canton, Sam. That's something you don't know about, and one of the main reasons I hunted you down this morning. I need to tell you about it. This is what I'm talking about when I said I learned something at the photograph place."

"She's not Julia Canton. Right. Right. I understand, amigo. I've been misunderstanding her name all this time."

"You know who her daddy was, Sammy?"

"Preacher out of Georgia."

"Uh-uh. Think again."

"Don't need to. She told me about him herself."

"She lied."

Heller stretched to his full height in his chair, fists clenching. "You watch that mouth of yours, Johnny. You might find yourself in the same shape as that hombre Julia hit with the offering plate in church: blowing your own teeth out your hind end!"

Johnny felt like yelling out what he had to say, but he realized that the words did not need to be broadcast on a public street, where unnoticed ears could overhear. So he drew in a few breaths, calmed himself, and spoke quietly. "Her daddy was Black Ear Skinner. Her name ain't Julia, but Della Rose. Della Rose Skinner, daughter of the old ash-eared devil hisself. And there's a picture of Black Ear's family down at Perkins's place that proves it. And now I've told you. My duty's done and I'm heading on my way."

Heller took it all in and rolled it around his mind, then chuckled. The chuckle grew into a full-out laugh.

"Black Ear's daughter! Baw-ha-ha-ha-ha-ha! Johnny Cross, I've heard bilge and bull come out of your mouth before, but never nothing to top that! Ha!"

Johnny Cross stared at him, silent and unshaken. "Believe what you want. I've seen the picture. But don't go asking Four-eye Perkins about it. It was Timothy Holt who showed it to me, and Perkins don't know he done it. Don't want to get the boy in trouble."

Heller's laughter subsided, but his mood of mockery did not. He cleared his throat and improvised a song to a familiar old fiddle tune. "Della Rose, Della Rose, she's the gal nobody knows! Flounces 'round and says she's Julia, but Johnny says she's trying to fool ya!"

Johnny Cross rolled his eyes sarcastically. "Good song, Sam. You ought to sing it to her while you swing her around at that dance."

"I may do that! Yep!"

"See you later, Sam. You take care, you hear?"

"I'll do that, Johnny. You do the same. Come up with something more believable next time. Black Ear Skinner. Ha!"

Thinking through it all later in the day, Sam began to worry despite himself. Much of the worry had to do with what Johnny Cross had said about unusual activity out where Heller ranged most of his longhorns. But there was another thing, too, something involving Julia that made Heller wonder if Johnny was onto something after all, wild as it sounded.

The picture in the Dog Star of the dead Black Ear gang member named Toleen. She'd known him. Identified him as Cal Toleen. And she'd seemed quite confident when she said it.

How could she have known such a man, and been so sure of it? How, indeed, as a mere preacher's daughter from Georgia?

It was early for it, but Heller needed a drink, bad. He headed for the Dog Star.

CHAPTER SEVENTEEN

Heller drank enough at the Dog Star to take the edge off his worries, but no more. He valued discipline too highly to let himself become one of those men who loses himself in a bottle. Sometimes folks who did that never found their way out again.

Leaving the Dog Star, he paused beside the picture of the dead man. "Cal Toleen, is that really you?" he muttered beneath his breath. "Or was she just talking through that blackberry wine she'd drunk, just blabbing her mouth?"

Cal Toleen had nothing to say in reply, so Heller moved on. Out on the street he pondered marching over to Otto Perkins's place and demanding to see that photograph Johnny Cross had talked about, but then he remembered what Cross had said about keeping Timothy out of trouble and decided he wouldn't chance it. The whole business was probably a hoax Cross had cooked up, but just in case it wasn't, he'd look out for Timothy. The poor dullard had enough troubles without having his newest boss down on him.

Should he simply go to the dress shop, pull Julia aside, and tell her what Johnny Cross was saying about her? That thought brightened his mood. If Johnny was indeed making up such a scandalous story, Julia would surely not take at all kindly to learning what a man she used to walk about town with, in public, was telling others about her. That would turn the tables on Johnny Cross, no doubt about it!

Heller had already begun trudging toward the dress shop when he made himself stop and think. Might the tables not turn right back on him if he went to her in a way that implied he gave credence to Cross's wild tale? Even if she despised Cross for making up a story about her heritage, and impugning her honesty, she might be just as disillusioned with Heller for being willing to consider it as possibly true.

Best to forget the whole Della Rose Skinner nonsense and think about the other part of what Cross had said: the thing about strange activity at Resurrection Gulch. Activity seemingly involving Heller's own cattle.

Heller readjusted his hat, checked to make sure he was carrying a decent supply of ammunition in his saddlebag, and began the ride out to the remains of the failed settlement.

* * *

Being unsure of what reaction he would provoke, the man waited until he knew the proprietress of the dress shop was absent on an errand before he went in. He entered with stealth, managing to reach a hand up and muffle the entrance bell above the door before it jangled. He eased the door closed and knew his quarry had no idea he was there.

He heard her before he saw her. She was coming from the back room, bearing a box of scissors ready to go on display for sale. He hid himself behind a tall shelf and let her get the scissors in their place. She stepped back to examine the display, and only then did he speak.

Using the same whispery voice he'd employed outside the boardinghouse window in the darkness so recently, he said, "Della Rose? Della Rose? It's time to come home now."

Her reaction was faster and more violent than he would have anticipated. She grabbed one of the scissors she'd just put on display and confronted him with the closed blades pointing like a knife. Startled, he back-stepped and looked pleadingly at her beautiful but intense face.

"Who are you, and what are you doing here?" she demanded. "And why did you call me by that name?"

"Della, please, please . . . I mean you no harm. There's no need to—"

"Why do you call me that? My name is Julia Canton! Who are you?"

"My name is Brody, Wilfred Brody. I am a detective, a man-hunter. In this case, a woman-hunter."

"Have you been looking for me? Watching me?"

"I have. And I apologize for my recent actions outside your boardinghouse, whispering and no doubt seeming threatening. That was my intent at that time. To unsettle you. I thought that might make it easier to persuade you to come home."

"What do you mean, come home?"

"Please put down the scissors, Della. Please."

"No. If I put them anywhere it will be through your throat! Why do you call me Della, and who sent you? You'd best speak up. If my employer returns and finds you here in this situation, she will have the law on you!"

"I call you Della because we both know who you really are. You are Della Rose Skinner. And I've come to bring you home because your mother needs you and has sent for you."

"'Sent for me.' What kind of fool do you think I am? My mother is unable to speak or even move. She has no power to 'send for me.' You are a fraud and a lecher, that's what I think! A man who watches young women where they work and where they live, and whispers at them from the dark!"

"Listen to me, Della. I understand your fear and confusion. But hear this: Your mother has awakened at last. She has come out of the stupor she has been in. It was unexpected, no sign of it happening until it did. She is weak, her speech is very slurred, and her vision and much of her movement is impaired, but she is back in the real world again, able to make her wishes known and understand what is happening around her. When she learned you had come to Texas, she hired me to come find you and bring you home."

"I don't believe you. It has been years—years!—since my mother was stricken. Why should I believe something has suddenly changed?"

"May I reach into my pocket and bring out something that may give what I say more credence?"

"Move slowly."

Brody reached beneath his vest and drew out a sealed envelope marked with a familiar design. Rose Skinner's personal emblem, used on all her personal correspondence in the years before her stroke. The man held it out and nodded.

She took it in trembling fingers and managed with one hand and her teeth to tear it open, never lowering the scissors with which she held the self-described detective at bay. She pulled the paper inside out with her teeth, dropped the envelope, and took the paper in hand. Holding it up where she could see the face of it and keep the man visible at the same time, she read it.

It was a quick read, just two words, scrawled so messily in pencil that they were nearly indecipherable. *DELLA HOME*

"You can see in how the letters look that it was a great strain for her to write," Brody said. "She has not used those muscles in many years. I, frankly, am surprised she was able to write at all."

Tears came, unwanted. She lowered the paper. "Why should I believe this? You or anyone else could have scrawled this out, making it look like the hand of someone who has been long afflicted, and using my mother's personal stationery."

"That is true, Della. It could have been faked. But that isn't what happened. I don't know what I can do to persuade you. All I can do is ask you to come home and see for yourself. I am prepared to accompany you."

"Ha! Me, traveling with you? That won't happen, Mr. Brody, though I wonder if that is your real name. I don't believe what you're telling me, and there are things holding me here that would make it impossible for me to leave even if I wished to. I have work here and much more lucrative and important work soon to come."

"I don't know what to say, Della. I thought that surely you would wish to rush home to a mother so long unavailable to you!"

"First, you can stop calling me Della. That is a name that used to be, but now I am Julia Pepperday Canton. I am from Georgia, just as Della was, and I had a brother with a similar limitation of mind as Della's late brother. But my father, my father, Julia's father, was a preacher. A good man. Not like Della's father, an outlaw."

Brody was relaxing a little, seeking to strengthen his hand in a situation that had gone not according to plan. He gave her a feigned look of sympathy and understanding. "From all I have heard, though, Della's father, though not what most would call a good man to all, was at least a good man to his younger daughter. He gave her education, opportunity. Freedom. Love."

"This discussion ends. I'm taking you to the law, and we'll see if you can persuade them with your words!" She shook the scissors and made a little lunge with them.

He was fast, faster than she would ever have anticipated. In half a moment her wrist was trapped in one of his hands while the scissors were being wrenched out of her fingers by the other. She cried out, but he anticipated it and pushed her face against his chest in a way that muffled her voice. She was fast disarmed, and then he had her firmly in his grasp.

"What are . . . what are you going . . ."

She did not finish her question. He tripped her and shoved her downward at the same moment. She went down hard, her head striking the edge of a heavy table. Without another sound she went limp and collapsed. He let her drop to the floor, knelt to make sure she was indeed unconscious, then picked her up as if she weighed nothing and carried her out of the store over his shoulder, like a sack of potatoes.

It was the first time he'd ever carried this particular young woman, but there'd been plenty of others, in other places. Women rendered senseless by violence, liquor, or opiates. Unlike many men who committed his particular favored crime, he was selective in his victims. If a man was going to risk hanging for the sake of taking his own pleasures, he might as well choose the best and most beautiful.

He'd had his eye on Della Rose Skinner since the time he'd seen her in the house of Black Ear Skinner, bringing in a fresh-picked flower to give to her mother, who, of course, knew nothing of it because she was a barely living, unconscious being, lying propped up on a pillow, eyes three-quarters closed and seeing nothing. Brody had been in that house at that time because Black Ear had come to suspect one of his former gang members had stolen from him, then fled, and Skinner needed a good man-hunter to locate him so that Skinner could see to the embezzler's proper punishment.

Brody had done the job, found the man, and conveyed to his employer word of how and where to capture him. Last Brody had heard of the fellow, he'd turned up dismembered in a dry gully somewhere up in the Nations. Evidence indicated some young Indian bucks had done the nasty work . . . but if so, Brody had known who paid them to do it.

The morally unrestrained man-finder had never forgotten Black Ear Skinner's lovely little girl. She had precisely the type of beauty that roused Brody's passions, and when Black Ear had shorted him on the pay promised for finding that thieving-and-fleeing gang member, Brody had made himself a promise. He'd not take the risk of trying to gouge the missing pay out of Skinner. He'd be patient, bide his time, and take his recompense in a far more gratifying way, with Black Ear's own beloved daughter, the one he valued, not the plain-faced one whom Skinner reportedly refused even to acknowledge as his own, despite her obvious dead-ringer similarity to him.

When word came at length that Black Ear Skinner had been shot through the head during a robbery in Mason, Texas, Brody had been infuriated. By dying, Black Ear had robbed Brody of the pleasure of seeing the outlaw realize that his own daughter had been ravaged by a man he'd cheated. Brody had been on the verge of giving up on the notion entirely, but when he thought back on the beauty of Della Rose Skinner, her flawless face and spilling chestnut hair, he envisioned pleasure and satisfaction that had nothing to do with Black Ear Skinner. Most likely, the dead Skinner had other things on his mind, considering where he surely had gone.

The long-standing plan to capture and take his pleasure with Black Ear's younger daughter had grown from a spark to a full flame within the depraved being of Wilfred Brody. He'd turned his man-hunting skills toward the finding of the young lady, and in the process learned something intriguing: the former gang members of Black Ear Skinner had scattered upon their leader's death, but now were beginning to move. All in the same direction, like a parade of bad men. Yet not exactly a parade, but more of a convergence. Something, or someone, was drawing them to a particular little spot in Texas. A remote, dusty smattering of adobe and wood and stone called Hangtree, famous only for its mass execution of renegade deserters during the Mexican-American War.

CHAPTER EIGHTEEN

Heller adjusted his field glasses and looked closely at the cattle in the rope corral nearest him. He was almost entirely certain that the brand he could barely make out over the distance was in fact his. He swept the glasses to the right and found a view of one of the men on horseback just outside the corral. He focused in and held the glasses steady, but the man was a stranger.

A rustling operation? Surely so, but Heller couldn't quite put together why it was being done in the way it was. The cattle were crowded together to an unreasonable degree, as if about to be herded onto cattle cars. But no railroad ran here.

Moving his field of view about some, he found another man on horseback, facing roughly in his direction. Heller adjusted the glasses and suddenly drew in his breath. On the back of the horse was a man with the same face as that which looked out in blind portraiture from the front corner of the Dog Star Saloon. Toleen!

This, of course, could not be the same man. It had to be his twin. If Julia had been right in identifying the dead one as Cal Toleen, that had to be Cal's twin brother, Drew, out there on horseback. Drew Toleen, killer, rapist, highwayman, cattle thief, bank robber.

Bank robber.

Heller put down the field glasses and thought hard. A memory of an old notion he'd developed when first getting to know the town of Hangtree came back to him. The flimsy nature of many of the buildings, mostly a mix of adobe and frame structures, had struck him. A good storm, a cyclone, a tremor of the earth, even a concentrated stampede . . . any of those things, it appeared, would have the potential to flatten Hangtree like a finger-flicked house of cards. It was easy to imagine the chaos and vulnerability that would result.

Especially if the last scenario was in play: a concentrated and even directed stampede. Waves of heavy bovine bodies surging and trampling and crashing . . . if it was fast enough and intense enough, the town could be brought down and its humanity driven into what cellars and surviving shelters remained.

At times, just for his own entertainment, Heller had toyed around with trying to figure out how, if he were criminally inclined, he might go about using a massive stampede as a cover for crime in Hangtree. With many hundreds of cattle devastating the town, why, a man could get away with murder, arson, robbery. Most of all, robbery.

Even a bank robbery.

He studied the scene before him and rubbed his chin, thinking and trying to put pieces together. It all seemed ludicrous and far-fetched . . . but far-fetched things were happening in Hangtree County lately, and obviously *something* unusual was going on.

On the remote chance that someone was actually setting up a bank robbery, Heller stood to lose a lot. No one would suffer more from a cleanout of the bank than would he.

Even without that, even if there was no stampede and no robbery, Heller and his fortune were in an imperiled situation here. His eye moved over to the abandoned ruin of the church where a crazed preacher had once declared the Confederacy would be magically reborn through the hand of God himself. He drew in a long, deep breath, and let it out slow.

There was a cellar beneath that ruined church. A cellar nearly inaccessible because of rubble that had collapsed into it. *Nearly* inaccessible, but not fully so. Someone who knew the way in, or even had the patience to explore until that way was ferreted out . . . that person or group of persons could put their hands on something Sam Heller himself had hidden away beneath that church years before. Something worth digging for.

Thousands of dollars in gold and silver. A buried treasure, not from some bandit or pirate's lost fortune, but the product of Sam Heller's hard and diligent work over a period of years.

Most of Sam's fortune was locked away in the Hangtree Bank, just like Arvil Caldwell liked it. But Heller had never been a man much trustful of overly formalized institutions. He believed much in the institution of law, but even there trusted the general principles of equity and the application of commonsense fairness and justice above the strictures of strict legalism. Heller had declined to assume that bankers in suits and vaults with heavy doors were necessarily the best way to keep a man's money safe. The problem was that everyone knew that banks were full of money, and that the money was locked up. And that locks could be opened and vaults emptied.

Heller looked at the church ruins through his field glasses and was pleased to see there was no evidence that anyone was poking around there just now, or that rubble had been shifted or removed. Whatever was going on at least had nothing to do with digging around beneath that church. He was mighty glad of it.

Heller crabbed backward until it was safe to stand without fear of being seen. He went to his hobbled horse and mounted, heading back to Hangtree.

So Johnny Cross had told him the truth when he described the goings-on out here at the ghost town. Might he also have been telling the truth about Julia actually being daughter to Black Ear Skinner?

And if she was, might the fact Della Rose Skinner was in Hangtree County account for the fact that old Black Ear stalwarts such as the Toleen brothers were here, too? Was she here because of them, or were they here because of her? Or was it mere coincidence?

Heller tilted back his hat and looked up past the brim to the sky. "Lord, you're going to have to help me figure this one out. Because right now I'm mighty, mighty perplexed, and I ain't going to deny it."

He rode on toward town, thoughtful and receiving no answers from either his own tumbling mind or the Lord above.

Jumbled items, a disheveled display, and a missing shop girl who had shown no prior evidence of unreliability. Those were the realities that initially disturbed Myrtle Bewley when she got back from her errand-running and found the dress shop open but empty.

What had Johnny Cross disturbed, though, was the combination of those same facts with the blood on the corner of a display table, with a little more pooled beneath it on the floor, drops leading back through the shop and out the door. Someone had injured himself or herself on that table, then had walked out through the shop's rear entrance.

Or been carried out.

Myrtle was distraught. "Oh, if something has happened to her because I left her alone here, I'll never forgive myself for it! Never! Such a sweet girl, and so pretty! If I'd had a daughter, I'd want her to be exactly like—"

"Try to calm down, Myrtle," Cross cut in. "We don't know yet what happened. Could have been a customer who fell and hurt themselves, and Della . . . Julia, I mean, maybe helped them out so they could get tended by the doc and didn't have a chance to close up. If that's the case, we'll know soon. Right now Clifton Smalls is out looking for the doctor to see if he's tending anybody with injuries that might match up with somebody falling against the corner of a tabletop."

"What if . . . what if she's . . ."

"If she, or anybody else who got hurt here, was dead, then they'd likely be lying either in the shop or out back somewhere, and there's no corpses about that I can see."

"No, but there's blood. It's the blood . . . It bothers me to see it . . ."

"I don't blame you for that, Myrtle. I don't like seeing it either. I hope just as much as you do that she's not hurt. Or nobody else either." He touched a fingertip to the blood on the edge of the tabletop. "Of course, it's pretty obvious that *somebody* is hurt."

Myrtle let out a wild wail, loud enough to hurt Cross's ears. He poked a fingertip into his nearer ear and jiggled it about, trying to reduce the ringing.

"I'm so sorry," Myrtle said. "I'm just so upset by this!"

"I have a suggestion," Johnny said. "Let's turn the sign over to say 'Closed,' and you get out of here for today. I'll make sure this blood gets cleaned up, and as soon as we get the good news that Della . . . Julia . . . is fine, I'll let you know right away."

"Why do you keep calling her by the wrong name?" Myrtle asked.

"I'm just loco, I reckon," Cross said, shrugging. "I had a dog name of Caleb when I was a boy, and once I called him Charlie for a day and a half. No reason for it. Just couldn't remember it right. Like I said, loco."

Cross's suggestion about closing shop was well-taken, and the act was done forthwith. Making Cross promise three times to run to give her news the instant it was received, Myrtle Bewley headed home, refusing to answer the queries of those who passed her and asked why she was crying. Once home she threw herself onto her big bed and sobbed until at last she fell asleep.

He was found behind the livery stable with a pitchfork thrust completely through his chest, the prongs coming out between his shoulder blades and pinning him to the earth like a bug in a schoolboy's classroom insect display.

No one knew him, but two or three people said they'd seen the man on the street, loitering about for the last two or three days, sometimes seeming to watch the dress shop and sometimes near the boardinghouse. "Some filthy fellow with wicked designs on that pretty shop girl, I'll betcha," said old Willie Walker, who had been leading the singing in the Hangtree Church the day that same and then-future "shop girl" had deprived a would-be thief of his teeth. "He dragged her out here and tried to have his way with her, and she got hold of that pitchfork and . . ." He grinned and nodded while making a jabbing motion, seemingly liking the violent vision running through his mind just then.

Sheriff Mack Barton had no better theories of his own, and so nodded at the old man. "Very well could be what happened, Willie. Could be. But you didn't actually see any of this yourself, right?"

"That's right. But I tell you, Sheriff, I'd be glad to testify to it in court all the same, 'cause that's pretty much the way it had to happen."

"I'm afraid it don't work that way, Willie. You can only testify to what you see."

The old man tapped the side of his head. "I can see it clear as a bell up here," he said.

"I'll let you know if we need you, then," Barton said. "Until then, keep a look out for that young woman. We found signs of a struggle over in the dress shop, and some blood on the corner of a table."

Willie Walker took that in and was troubled. He nodded grimly and shuffled off.

Deputy Clifton Smalls stepped up beside Barton and looked down at the corpse. "Reckon who he is?" he asked.

"I don't think he's going to be able to tell us," the sheriff replied.

"Like as not," said Smalls, nudging the corpse with his boot toe. "Like as not."

CHAPTER NINETEEN

She didn't know where she was or how she'd gotten here. The ceiling above her, the walls around her, the bed on which she lay, the cheap picture of a very Gentile Jesus hanging beside the bed . . . none of it was familiar. All she knew was she had awakened here, that the bed was comfortable, and her head hurt badly.

Lying in silence, sometimes hearing what might be the movement of someone elsewhere in this unknown house, Della Rose Skinner could remember only one time her head had throbbed so badly. She'd been riding with her father across Georgia pastureland, one of those rare days when the law had been compensated to look the other way and he wasn't being forced to hide so much as usual. She'd taken a spill when she'd unwisely tried to follow her father's instruction and example in jumping a rail fence. The fence wasn't particularly high, but Della was no good horseman at that age, and the horse had lost footing when it came down on the far side of the fence. Della Rose had been thrown from the saddle and banged her head on a stone. She'd awakened to find her father kneeling beside her, his mangled black ear even blacker for being silhouetted against the sky. He'd stroked her brow gently and told her that when it came to doing what he told her to, like jumping a horse before it, or she, were ready, it would be best if she exercised some restraint and common sense. He was not a good man for providing examples and instruction, he told her.

Thinking back on that old memory seemed to clear the way for more immediate remembrances to return. She recalled being surprised in the dress shop by a stranger who knew who she really was and made the extraordinary claim that he had been sent by Della Rose's own mother, purportedly newly awakened from her long coma, and that she should come with him and go home again to see the woman who had not laid eyes on her beloved daughter since she was a growing little girl.

There had been argument, resistance, struggle, and somehow she had fallen and hit her head on something in the shop. After that it was all a murk. A sense of being carried like a dead thing, of hearing the man who had her talking as if to himself, but talking *about* her, and saying things that filled her with dread and an understanding of his true reasons for seeking her out. She recalled being dumped on her back on the ground, her head hurting like all torture as the back of it slammed the hard earth, then her clothing being tugged at and the man laughing and sneering above her, telling her his intentions. His hands had groped and pushed and pressed, and she had been unable to fight them off . . .

Then suddenly he was gone, snatched away as if some great eagle had swept down from the sky and picked him up in its talons and carried him off. She'd passed out a few moments, then came groggily around to find a fight under way, her captor struggling with a man who seemed familiar but whom she could not immediately place. Whoever he was, he was her hero at that moment.

She'd moved a little, thinking of trying to sit up, when she'd spotted the pitchfork. It leaned against the horizontal boards making up the side of a barn or stable stall—it was then she recognized she was in the Hangtree livery stable—and she pulled herself toward it and used it to pull herself creakingly to her feet, where she wobbled a few moments while using the pitchfork as a crutch, its prongs rooted in the dirt of the livery floor. The fight went on, about ten or twelve feet from her. Her impression was that the fighting men were so engrossed in their combat that they did not even notice she had managed to stand.

So dizzy, so wobbly . . . she felt at that time as if she might never stand up easily again. Reaching up with her left hand, she touched the part of her head that hurt most and found broken skin and scabbing blood. She'd seen the open livery door and felt the urge to flee to the street and find help . . . but she knew she could not flee if she could not even keep her own footing. Then one of the fighters nearby yelled in pain and she managed to turn and look.

The man who had captured her had gotten the arm of her would-be rescuer in his grip and was twisting it so severely she was sure the bone would snap and poke right out through his flesh. She looked at the man's face and suddenly remembered where she'd seen him before.

He'd been behind the pulpit the day she had made herself locally famous with the help of a heavy wooden collection plate in the Hangtree Church. It was the preacher himself, the Reverend Fulton, if memory served correctly regarding his name, and obviously he'd seen her being carried into the livery by her captor and had been brave enough to react.

Fulton was a heavier man than the one he was fighting, the supposed Wilfred Brody, but Brody possessed more skill and youth. Fulton was taking the worst of it. Della saw that if the scenario didn't change, Brody would prevail, Fulton would be hurt or killed, and she would be in just as bad a captive position as before.

But there was no one to help. No one but she, and she was so woozy as to hardly be able to move, much less fight.

A horrible, muffled splintering noise, and a

new scream of suffering from Fulton, told her that the preacher's arm was indeed fracturing.

From somewhere inside, a rage beyond anything she had ever felt had surged in Della Rose. Ignoring dizziness and wavering vision, she had raised the pitchfork and half-ran, half-staggered at the combatants. For a fraction of a moment Fulton's pain-filled eyes had met hers and she could tell he understood what she was doing. He'd exerted in one last burst of effort and managed to save his arm from further damage, but more importantly, to throw Brody off-balance and make him lose his grip on the fighting preacher.

When Brody stumbled a little, the opportunity came and she seized it without thought, hesitation, or any specific plan. Brody fell back against one of the support uprights that reached from the dirt floor to the base of the loft above. His arms flailed reflexively to the side, leaving his chest open and unprotected. Della stabbed with the pitchfork and struck home, though only penetrating a couple of inches. The pain of it was sufficient to drop Brody to his knees, though, giving Fulton time to break fully away from him, stumbling off while gripping and gingerly rubbing his twisted arm.

Della pulled the pitchfork back and then stabbed forward again, much harder. Brody's eyes had their death-glaze even as he was driven backward, his shoulders winding up between his own heels and the pitchfork pinning him to the ground. Della heard his hips popping out of joint even as he died, his hands moving in circles in the air above him, then flopping down and lying still at his sides.

Fulton, recovering some, came to the dead man and looked down on him. "Who was he?" he asked Della.

"He was a man who said he was paid to come and find me and take me home to my mother, who has been in a coma for years, to tell me she had awakened and had sent him to find me and bring me home to her."

"Good news, it would seem, Miss . . . Miss Pepperday. Do I remember your name rightly?"

"That is the name I gave, yes, or part of it. I go by Julia, my first name. Your memory is good, Reverend. I remember you, too . . . you are the fine preacher of the Hangtree Church."

"Not so fine the day you visited, Miss Pepperday. It was a day I felt a failure as a preacher of the divine word. It was a day of . . . struggle for me." Without a conscious effort to do so, he flicked his eyes for half a second down to her ample bosom and back up again.

"Will I hang, Reverend?" she asked, looking down at the pitchforked man.

"No, miss. No. You saved my life and probably your own. It was a defensive act, and no court in Texas would condemn you for it. Do you know what his name was?"

"He said it was Wilfred Brody. Probably a false

name." *I know all about false names*, she might have added.

"Probably. Do you think he was telling the truth regarding your mother?"

"I don't think so."

"So his goal was . . . something different, obviously."

"I think he had wicked intentions. Fleshly intentions. It isn't the first time I have encountered such things." Her mind flashed back to a time as a little girl when one of her father's associates attempted to put his hands on her in a most vulgar way. Black Ear Skinner caught him and relieved those hands of all ten fingers, one butcher knife chop at a time.

One thing Della had known all her life was that her father, though not a good man, was thoroughly devoted to her and her protection. She would admire that always about Black Ear Skinner, regardless of the wicked things said about him and attributed to him.

"You are a lovely young lady, Julia. I am sure that the blessing of beauty also brings its own curses as well, especially that of unwanted and wrongful attentions."

"It is true, Reverend. It is true." She frowned down at the corpse. "Should we tell someone?" Then she staggered, stabbed with pain that throbbed through her injured head.

"I'm getting you to medical help, Julia. You took a hard blow to the skull. Did he strike you?"

"I fell . . . against a table, I think. In the dress shop."

"You might have died from such an accident."

"I don't think it was an accident. I think he pushed me down."

"Come on, Julia. My house is not far and my wife, Claireen, can give you good care. She worked in military hospitals during the war. I will fetch the doctor in to see you there, and you may stay with us until you are steadier on your feet. The last thing we would want would be for you to fall again."

"You are a good man, Reverend. I've known good men and wicked ones in my life, and you are a good one."

"I hope I am. Thank you."

He led her out the rear of the livery stable, thinking it might look strange for people to see the local minister propping up a bloodied young beauty coming out of an enclosed and mostly windowless building. Around a few corners and down two alleys, and they reached his house. She had only the thinnest memory of meeting Claireen Fulton and of being guided into a spare bedroom and tucked away. Reverend Fulton had left to find the local doctor while Claireen had gently washed the crusted injury and then helped change her unexpected houseguest from her clothing into one of Claireen's own cotton shift nightgowns. After that Della Rose/Julia Pepperday's recollections were mostly absent, until she had awakened to find herself looking up at

that vaguely disturbing image of Jesus hanging
on the wall beside the bed.

"It might have been best had she been kept
awake as much as possible after the concussion of
her brain," said the same physician who had lost
one Hiram Tate on his surgical table while falling
short of removing a blasted arm that had been
barely hanging on anyway. Preacher Fulton had
found the bachelor doctor in his little residence,
pulling on a bottle of gin, and hustled him home
to have a look at Julia Canton's injuries. "Then
again," the doctor went on, "others say that sleep
is actually more helpful than wakefulness. It is a
debate in medicine that is likely to go on for some
time yet. In any case, I can say our lovely young
friend here seems on her way to recovery. It was a
nasty blow and an ugly cut on the brow, but I see
no reason to think this one will not be back on
her feet and living normally within days."

"What about dancing?" asked the patient. "I've
been invited to the town dance."

"No dancing, not that soon," said the doctor,
earning himself a piercing glare in return. "You
won't be steady enough for it, and there is simply
no need to take that risk."

With skull and brain pounded, she was in a
state of identity flux, alternately feeling more like
Julia Canton and then more like Della Rose Skinner. At news she would not be able to step out to

the music with the handsome Sam Heller, the Della Rose side won out.

Lying back against her pillow, she glared at the ceiling and said, "Damn. Damn to hell! I'm sorry, Preacher, I know that's not how you speak in this house, but . . . *damn!* I was invited and I was *so* looking forward to it."

Claireen and the doctor had stepped to the other side of the room for a moment to discuss aspects of the injured one's care, so Preacher Fulton drew a little closer to the bed, reached down and took one of her hands in his, and said, softly, "Don't fret, dear. Sometimes you encounter those situations in life where all you can do is just say"—he glanced quickly back at the others, then sharply whispered—"*damn.*" He squeezed her hand. He smiled at her and shifted his eyes heavenward. "I think the Maker understands his creatures and makes all proper allowances for their trivial failures, including those of saying what they, what *we*, shouldn't. I really think he does. I hope so. I do hope so."

Della Rose Skinner closed her eyes again and let herself slip back off into sleep. She dreamed, vividly, and in the dream she was dancing with Sam Heller beneath the Texas stars. No dizziness, no pain on or in her skull, no halting or stumbling of her feet. She spun in his arms, and for once it didn't matter whether she was Julia Pepperday Canton or Della Rose Skinner. She was simply herself and it was enough.

CHAPTER TWENTY

The dead man in the livery generated far less public interest than he might have in other towns. For one thing, he was a stranger, known to no one at all that anyone at all could seem to find. And generally speaking, unknown meant unimportant. Secondly, dead strangers were not all that uncommon in Hangtree. More than one local who heard that a corpse had been found pitchfork-pinned to the floor of the livery stable had shrugged and said, in effect, "Well, it's been a few weeks. 'Bout time somebody was kilt."

The late Wilfred Brody, after being photographed by Otto Perkins with pitchfork still in place through his torso, was beneficiary of a tradition that had come to be called in Hangtree a "good riddance funeral," the sort reserved for the most morally loathsome and despised dead. Such as strangers who came into town and made an apparent attempt to abduct and misuse the town's prize beauty. A round hole about a yard across was dug to a depth of five or six feet in a lesser corner of the Boot Hill burying ground, Brody was crumpled up and dumped on his rear in in a seated posture, sans coffin and even clothing, and a wagonload of longhorn dung was hauled in to begin the filling of the grave. Brody was submerged in half-liquid bovine filth, with only the top two feet of his grave filled with dirt, and that mostly just to hide the smell of the dung. No cross was put on his Boot Hill grave, just a crude sign made by a county prisoner under the oversight of Sheriff Barton and Deputy Smalls. The sign read simply: HERE RESTS A BAD MAN. It's what they would have inscribed even if they'd known his name. Three other graves with an identical inscription were nearby—other despised souls who met their ends, in all cases violently, in Hangtree.

Faithful to his calling, Reverend Fulton came out and pronounced the only funeral oration the unfortunate Brody would receive. Preacher Fulton closed his eyes beside the filled hole, lowered his head, and intoned, "God be merciful to the departed sinner here buried." It was his standard liturgy for "good riddance burials." Otto Perkins posed and took a photograph of the preacher and the delegation of volunteer gravediggers (most of them drunk), standing by the filled hole with the emptied manure wagon sitting to the side, and that was that for Wilfred Brody, failed rapist.

Of more interest to most Hangtree folk than the passing of one more piece of stray human trash was how badly the town's most lovely lady had been treated and hurt by that particular scoundrel. It was known about Hangtree that she had been going to attend the town dance with Sam Heller, but that her injury was going to prevent her from taking part. Because she had become something of a living town mascot and heroine since her escapade at the church service, not to mention the adored embodiment of female beauty because of her many walks about town and her generally friendly manner with those who greeted her, Hangtree's people took it seriously that she had been harmed. To have been very nearly carried away and misused by a depraved stranger lent an aura of romantic tragedy to Julia Canton that couldn't have been heightened short of her actual death at the hands of the degenerate, or her rescue by her perceived suitor, Sam Heller, rather than the local parson.

It wasn't that the locals had given up their widespread deploring of Heller's "carpetbagger" status. It was that romantic tragedy covered a multitude of sins. Even, to some degree, carpetbagging.

Ironically, Julia's head injury and the temporary immobility it inflicted upon her might have saved her life, most locals concluded as the facts came out. If she had not suffered the blow to her head and her captor had been able to force her at gunpoint to travel with him, he might have gotten her away quickly to some hidden place, where only all-seeing God would have envisioned the atrocious things that would have been done to her . . . God, that is, in company with the drunken degenerates at the Dog Star Saloon. The same lechers who came to watch knicker-shunning Petunia Scranton doing the high-kicking can-can to the sped-up tune of a camp meeting hymn could imagine in vivid detail the perverse things that might have been inflicted upon Julia Canton, and they talked them over without the slightest restraint among themselves, reveling in the sordid visions their minds contrived.

There was some reaction to the crime against Julia Canton that was more than lust-driven imaginations on the part of local drunks. To maintain a smattering of law and order in a town with little of either, a coroner's jury was convened and the passing of Wilfred Brody was put down to "death by misadventure." That was, presumably, the misadventure of having a pitchfork rammed through his chest by a young woman he'd been about to rape.

Beyond that not-quite-real coroner's jury, the world of law and justice would have no more dealings with Wilfred Brody. It was ready to forget him. Eternally seated in his narrow hole on Boot Hill, encased in steaming, decaying dung, he was where he belonged.

Claire Fulton had learned and accepted the fact that a preacher is eternally at the beck and call of the people he serves, and that the same is true for his wife. It was her job to set the proper example of compassion and caring for someone who was wronged and hurt, so she did it. It was clear to all that Julia Canton was better off under Claire Fulton's care in the parsonage than she would be in her own rented room at the boardinghouse, so the contents of her wardrobe were cleaned out at the boardinghouse and shifted to one in the corner of the Fultons' spare room, now Julia's chamber.

Claire fell back on her old wartime training-through-experience as a nurse and began to thoroughly enjoy having someone to care for. She kept a close eye on Julia's wounded head, and comforted her with assurances that there would be little scarring (though in reality she worried that there would). She was pleased that Julia seemed to be feeling better first by the day, then by the hour. The doctor began to allow her more movement, assuming Claire was by her side to keep her from succumbing to the dizziness that appeared likely to be a lingering problem for a while.

Visitors began to call, a mixed blessing for Julia because she cherished her privacy, and because several of her visitors were local young men who obviously were looking for a way to meet the prettiest girl in town. She was kind to them, but not talkative, and most got the message and left quickly.

She was napping one afternoon when the bedroom door opened and closed and Claire was there, followed by the enticing scent of the stew she was cooking downstairs. She slipped to the bedside and made her usual inquiries about how Julia was feeling and gave the usual quick check to her bandage. Then she took up a hairbrush from the bedside table and gave Julia's hair a quick fixing-up. "Much better, much better! Though I have to say, most of us would love to have hair that retained so much thickness and form after going unwashed for days. Me, my hair is a pancake against my noggin after a single night's sleep. But look at you! All beauty and brightness no matter what."

"It's because I have such a good caregiver looking out for me."

"It's my delight, dear. It has brightened my week to have you with me, even under such dark-edged circumstances."

"You spoil me, Claire. You truly do."

"Oh! I almost forgot: The town dance was to be tomorrow night, but it has been put off for a week to make sure you have time to recover and take part. It was Mayor Holloman who came up with the idea, and the town fathers were quick to say yes. They want to give you special honor in the dance. The entire town sees you as a hero for the brave way you stood up to that thief in church, and how you fought so hard against that dreadful man who hurt you, and bested him."

"I couldn't have done so without your husband."

"I want to ask you to tell him that. Not immediately, and not in any way that seems to be deliberate, if you know what I am trying to say. Just when you are having a conversation sometime."

"Is something wrong?"

Claire sighed and looked across the bed and out the window. "It's hard to know how to say it. His church was intruded by an armed robber while he was standing in the pulpit, and he did nothing to stop it. Then a little slip of a girl, armed with nothing but an offering plate and a steel nerve, brings the entire situation to an end. Then, when he finds that same slip of a girl being attacked and steps in to try to rescue her, as any good man would, it ends up being the girl herself who defeats the attacker. Very dramatically, I must say."

"That would not have happened if Preacher Fulton hadn't first pulled the man off me. I can assure you of that."

"Let him hear you say it sometime."

"I will."

"Men have a certain kind of pride, you know. It is their greatest weakness, that pride. And with it goes some degree of cruelty. Men say things to one another to attack the pride of one another."

"And local men have been gigging him for letting a female win his battles for him. Not that I'm saying I see it that way . . . I'm just trying to guess what is prompting you to say these things. He's being mocked, isn't he?"

"He is. And he tries to shake it off and say it doesn't matter, that God despises pride in a man and he must shun it . . . but even so, even so . . ."

Julia sat up a little straighter, leaning back against the headboard. It hurt her much less this time to do it, and roused much less dizziness. When she was settled, she said, "Claire, Preacher Fulton is perhaps the finest man I've known. I give him credit for my life. And if this town plans to honor me in some public way, they'd best be prepared to hear me give equally public credit to the man who pulled a debaucher off of me, a man who very nearly killed me by throwing me down against the sharp edge of a hardwood table. I'll not have anyone diminishing such a fine and brave gentleman on my account."

Tears had actually formed in Claire's eyes. "Thank you, dear. Thank you."

A knock sounded downstairs, someone at the outer door. Claire jumped up and quickly wiped her eyes. "Another caller for you, I suspect. Are you up to another visitor?"

"Send them up. I can always influence people to leave by pretending to go to sleep, if I must."

"Clever child, you are! Clever child!"

CHAPTER TWENTY-ONE

The caller at the door was a man probably in his fifties, and he asked if he might have a chance to talk to his niece for a few moments. He gave his name as Cale Pepperday. Claire bid him wait a moment and dashed up the stairs.

"She says she'll see you, and asked me to give you some privacy so you can talk about family. I told her of course it was all right. May I bring you some coffee up, Mr. Martin?"

"Fine as I am, ma'am. I'll not be long with her."

"So, girly, tell me how you are doing."

"Well enough, I suppose. I tend toward headaches now."

"From the size of that bedsheet folded up on your topknot, I'd guess you took a sizeably hard blow."

"I lived through it."

"And he didn't."

"I got him with pitchfork prongs."

"You always were an enterprising one, child. When you were nine or ten, you were just like your mother was at that age."

"Uncle Cale, did you know the man who hurt me?"

"Tell me his name. I ain't heard it."

"He called himself Wilfred Brody. He claimed to be a hired manhunter, sent to find me. Sent by Mother."

Martin's expression had changed the moment he heard the name of Brody. His teeth clenched together behind his thin and bewhiskered lips, a habit he had when angry, and one Julia had known since her childhood as Della Rose.

"Lying son of a bitch!" Martin growled. "Wicked devil, that man! Pure wicked!"

"Could it be true? He said she'd come out of her—"

"Listen to me, Della Rose . . . she's gone. She passed on, peaceful they say, not long after you left."

Tears rose and trailed down a beautiful face and across trembling lips.

"Sorry to tell you, girly. I reckon I should have told you before, but it's been for so long as if she was dead anyway, there didn't seem much call to distress you over it."

"It's all right, Uncle Cale. It is. If she's gone, she's gone, and like you said, she's been gone a long time already."

"I miss her. Fine woman, my sister was. But she married bad."

"I know. Papa did wrong things. But you got to remember, Uncle Cale . . ."

"That I followed right along and joined in with him. Yep, I know that, girly. And now with Curry gone, here I am still doing it. Still planning to, anyway. That's part of why I come to see you today. I got to learn where all this stands now."

"I would think I could ask the same question of you."

"You can. And I can tell you that on my end of things, we're ready to go. We've just been waiting for you to come tell us when to get it started. And if this is going to be done, it can't wait much longer. I know the cattle have been seen, by who I don't know, but there's been men spotted watching and looking. Raises a lot of questions for folks, I reckon. That ain't your usual throwed-together herd of mavericks, most of them. Them's branded cattle for the most part. All kinds of brands, but most bear the Heller brand. What's going to happen is that somebody is going to decide what's going on is some kind of big rustling operation. Or if they are savvy enough to know a bit of history, they may figure out the truth, that this is a stampeder plan."

She nodded and said nothing.

"Let me just get right to the heart of it and ask you straight out, Della Rose: you still want to do this? We could turn them cattle back out loose on the plains as easy as you please, and go our way and be done with it. You'd have some mighty angry men on your hands, though. They see this one as something big, bigger, maybe, than most of what they did when your daddy was still leading them. They won't turn away easy. Might not turn away at all, no matter what you say."

Her manner changed when he said that. "Tell me what you mean by that."

"All right. All right, I will. You ain't going to like hearing it, I don't think."

"Talk!"

"Fine. Let's just run through it from the start. What we're doing here is getting ready to revive the Black Ears, and revive 'em big. This time with somebody different at the head of it all . . . you. Black Ear Skinner's own born daughter, his pride and joy. Taking up what her daddy had to leave behind when a bullet caught him in Mason. And besides reviving the gang, we're going to make us a piss-pot full of cash and gold, courtesy of Mr. Rich Man Carpetbagger Sam Heller of Hangtree, Texas. Right?"

"That's right."

"And we're going to go about this from two . . . no, three . . . angles. We know that Heller ain't a totally trusting man . . . he's got lots of money but don't trust banks to keep it all. So he puts only a part of it in the bank here. The rest he puts . . . well, nobody knows for sure. But the figuring is, if anybody could get Heller to let the cat out of the poke, it'd be a pretty lady who gets close enough to him. That being you."

"Right."

"Has that happened? Have you cuddled up enough with him to get him to talk?"

"We kind of got interrupted, you know."

"By Brody, you mean."

"That's right. By Brody, and a smashed head."

"Forget all that a moment. Let's move ahead. The plan is, you find out where Heller hides his money that ain't in the bank, and how to get to it. Second part of the plan, we stampede that big herd of cattle we've been collecting up out there right through this town and pound it to splinters. Meanwhile, with the town having its hands full with the cattle running everything and everybody into the dirt, we get into that bank and clean it out. Everything Sam Heller has becomes ours . . . property of the back-to-life Black Ears, and their leader, Della Rose Skinner. That's the plan."

"When you spell it out like that, it sounds . . . sounds . . ."

"Loco? Yeah, it does. Except that it's been done before. Little settlement over in East Texas, stampede tore through it three years ago, just an accident . . . and while the town was getting run over, some smart old boys there got the notion of cleaning out the local bank vault, which was standing open when the cattle came through, and also the stock of a gunsmith shop and a silversmith, all in the same town. They did it, got away clean, and never got caught. Happened there, it can happen here, with the difference being that the stampede happens when and how we want it to."

"If we can get all the advance work set up."

"The cattle are in place. And skittish. It ain't going to take much to stampede them. We got to get the rest of this in place, too, and move soon. And I mean real soon."

"I can't even stand up for long without holding to something for balance," she said. "And lying up here in this bed I ain't in much position to be galivanting around with Sam Heller to persuade him to tell me where he keeps his fortune."

"Hate to say this to my own sister's daughter, but if you can't galivant around with Heller out there, maybe he can do some galivanting with you up here."

She couldn't believe what she was hearing, not out of moral offense, but because of the sheer impracticality of it. "Uncle Cale, you'd best remember what 'up here' is. This is the spare bedroom in the local preacher's house. Neither Sam Heller nor anyone else is going to be allowed to come up here and 'galivant' with me in a parsonage bedroom."

"Then you'd best be figuring up another way to go about it, and fast. The cattle ain't the only thing getting restless out there. I got a bunch of men starting to ask why we really need a 'play-pretty girl' running this, anyway. They respect the memory of your father and the name of the Black Ears . . . but they don't see that this couldn't be done for the most part by them alone. Even if the money Heller keeps hidden somewhere is never found, there's still enough money in the Hang-tree Bank to make it worthwhile. And the stampeding you wouldn't be part of, anyway. They can pick their time, run them cattle in, and get that bank robbed at gunpoint before the local law can even see through the stampede dust."

"But that would be wrong. This isn't just another bank robbery. This is for my father, for his memory and his legacy. It has to be led by a Skinner to mean what it should mean."

Martin shook his head. "Girly, listen to your uncle. The men out there rode with your father and backed him up to the end. They were proud to be Black Ears with the original Black Ear himself. The point of all this being that they ain't doing this for the same reasons you are. For you it's family pride and a daughter picking up where her father was forced to leave off. For them, it's a job. A strike. Money to be got. They ain't going to wait much longer to reach out and take it."

Her heart was racing in her chest and it was hard to breathe. For the first time she wondered if this was going to happen, at least with her involved. Everything felt like a train about to jump track, and she had no idea what to do about it. Not while she was still laid up.

"Brody's fault, that's what it is. If he hadn't come along . . ."

"But he did come along, Della. Just a sorry devil your father made the mistake of hiring one time. And I reckon Brody must have took a shine to you, the wrong kind, and there you are."

"Tell them it will be soon, Uncle Cale. Tell them to be patient just a little while longer, and keep a look out for trouble. And before you know it the ground will be shaking and cattle will be rumbling by, and what's in that bank vault right now will be in their saddlebags. *Our* saddlebags."

"I'll tell them. I don't know how much they'll listen. There's been talk lately of another way, maybe an easier way. There's a banker, name of Caldwell. He's in a position to be pressured. He could get us in, get us access to the vault . . ."

"Do what you have to, then. But remember who it is who is running this thing. And Uncle Cale . . . who is it who is stirring things up?"

"I ain't going to say, girly. Nothing gained by it." And without saying anything more, he was gone.

Julia felt very tired all at once. Closing her eyes, she fell asleep propped up against the headboard.

"What are you thinking, Cale?" asked Drew Toleen of Cale Pepperday after his return from visiting his niece.

"Drew, I hate to say it, but I don't believe we're going to be able to wait on her anymore. She says she wants to go on, but I don't know. Something ain't right. Maybe she's got cold feet, or is getting religion, or just getting scared . . . but I think this thing is either going to be done by us, fast, or not done at all. Just my gut feeling, but I ain't usually wrong."

"When, then?"

"They got a big town dance coming up in two nights. I say let them dance theirselves ragged and crawl off late to bed, then hit the next morning when they're still wore out. Get it done and get out of town."

"What about the vault? How will we get it open?"

"It'll be open. Don't fret."

CHAPTER TWENTY-TWO

Sam Heller, plagued by doubts raised by the things Johnny Cross had told him about the Skinner family picture in Otto Perkins's studio, had put off paying a call on Julia Canton, choosing instead to quietly check in with Myrtle Bewley, who was dropping in to see Julia regularly, and other times getting information from Claire Fulton. He knew that he would be driven to put the question to her directly if he sat down with her: are you Julia Pepperday Canton, or are you Della Rose Skinner?

Heller wasn't afraid of much, but personal confrontations of that sort distressed him. His affection for Julia made him loathe to endanger his relationship with her, something he feared a direct question might do. So he hung fire, walking and riding past the parsonage where she resided at the moment, but never going to the door.

Until now. He simply couldn't wait. The postponed town dance was two nights away, and the town was expecting him to escort the lovely Julia Canton. He couldn't leave the matter unsettled.

So it was he strode now toward the parsonage, flowers in hand and making him feel so foolish that he tried to hide them with his body, a task of course not fully achievable. Still worried about how a direct question regarding her identity might be received, he decided to simply let conversation progress where it would.

Claire Fulton greeted him quite politely and offered him coffee and a vase for his flowers when he came in. He accepted both. After a few minutes of strained conversation, he was left alone while Claire went upstairs to make sure her houseguest was in a position to receive company.

She came downstairs and Heller started up with flower vase in hand. Claire stopped him and suggested he leave his mule-leg on the mantelpiece, it not seeming a fitting item to carry on a visit to an injured young woman. Heller complied and handed the weapon down to Claire, who accepted it in a manner suggesting she thought it might bite her.

The reunion was as clumsy as Heller had feared, but Julia's warm manner eased the strain substantially. Heller was glad to learn that she remained pleased to accompany him to the dance, and the conversation became amusing as she described to him a visit from Hilda Farley the day before. Hilda told her that her husband, Claude, had composed a piece of fiddle music he called the "Brave Maiden Waltz," dedicated to her. It was his intention to play it while she and Heller waltzed before the attendees.

"Oh no, no . . . I ain't no trained circus bear, some dancing critter in a show tent. I ain't even sure I know how to waltz, Julia."

"We can practice. Right now."

"You ain't supposed to be doing such, are you?"

"That was right after I was hurt. I'm fine for it now, as long as I don't trip and fall."

"You start planting them dainties of yours down where my big old paddles are slapping the floor, trip and fall is just what you'll do."

Clad in her nightgown and a modest white robe borrowed from her hostess, Julia got out of bed. Heller held her hand to steady her, and they simply walked about the floor a few moments, letting her get past the dizziness that still plagued her. She did so swiftly, and began to hum an old waltz tune, breaking up the music with instruction on the art of dancing in three-quarter time.

The bedroom door remained open at Claire's instruction. As the wife of the local parson she found it important that wrong perceptions be avoided. But as they waltzed about the relatively small open space on the floor, Heller inevitably tapped the door and it closed. When Claire did not appear and reopen it at once, they relaxed and waltzed a little faster to Julia's hummed music.

"See?" Julia said as he held her close. "You can do it! And so can I . . . I'm not falling over or even feeling very dizzy."

"I won't lie to you, Julia. I could go on holding

on to you like this all day long, I think. And maybe through the night, too. Am I wrong in speaking so?"

"I'm not offended in the slightest. But I do feel all at once like I might fall. Help me lie down . . . I'm dizzy."

He held her steady and moved her back to the bed, where she sat down, looking peaked. He looked closely at the white bandage skillfully emplaced on her head by Claire Fulton, and saw no sign of fresh blood penetrating.

"I think I should lie down now," she said.

"We may have to pass on the dancing at the big play-party," Heller said. "Claude can play his new waltz and everybody else can have at it, but I think you may need to recover a little longer before you get out there swinging about and all. Don't you think so, Della?"

They both froze rigid at his calling of that name. She looked at him with eyes wide and jaw fixed, and he felt like the world's most bumbling fool.

He hadn't planned to call that name. He'd lost himself sufficiently in the dance and the closeness of her that the whole matter of her name had been nearly forgotten. But now that it was out it was out. He looked at her and tried to read her expression.

"Why did you call me that?" she asked weakly.

"I didn't plan to . . . it just came out."

"But why? Why that name?"

"Does the name mean something to you?"

"What it means to me is that you're here with me, but there's someone else on your mind. Someone named Della."

There seemed little point in dodging now. "Della Rose Skinner, to be exact."

He felt her tense, body flinching up hard as flint. "Who?"

"Maybe you know."

"Sam, what are you talking about? Why are you . . ."

"I'm told there is a picture of the family of Black Ear Skinner right here in this town. Taken some years back. And in that picture is . . . you."

"That's absurd! Why would I be in a picture of some outlaw's family?"

"What I'm told is that it's because maybe you were part of that family. That your real name is Della Rose Skinner, and Julia Canton was a name made up to use in place of the real one."

She spluttered and seemed authentically stunned. "Why would . . . how can . . . who is it telling you these tales?"

"Folks who are generally to be relied upon."

"Where is this picture? I want to see it."

"I ain't got it. I ain't even seen it. But one who has tells me there's no mistake. It's a younger gal in the picture, but the gal is you, clear as morning."

"It's nonsense! My name is Julia, not Della whoever! How could you believe anything different? I told you myself who I am. You think some old picture can change my identity? My history? Whoever is in that picture, it isn't me. Somebody else. Take my word!"

"That's all the word I've got to go by. On the other side, though, there's the fact that somebody who can be trusted on such things swears that picture shows you."

"You're simply choosing to believe someone else over me, then?"

"There's more to it than that. Tell me something, Julia. How was it you were so sure in naming that Toleen brother in that picture at the Dog Star as being Cal Toleen? How would Julia Pepperday Canton, preacher's daughter from Georgia, know one outlaw twin from the other?"

"I . . . didn't. I was just talking. It was just something to say."

"Mighty odd thing to say just to be saying, don't you think?"

"Maybe it was. I suppose I thought it would make me sound like I knew important things. I don't know! I just said it."

"Don't cry on me now, Julia. I don't like it when women cry on me."

She clenched her teeth at him. "And I don't like being called a liar and told I'm the daughter of an outlaw, when I know perfectly well who I am!"

Sam had expected this might go badly. And it was. For a few moments there was nothing but silence between them. Then a sudden light rap on the bedroom door, and a slightly alarmed Claire Fulton opened the door and peered in, her alarm stemming from the fact they were together, in her house and the church's house, in a bedroom with the door closed.

When she saw them both sitting on the bed, she blanched. "Julia? Are you all right?"

"Fine, Claire. I'm fine. *We're* fine. Nothing for you to worry about here."

Sam stood. "I'd best be going."

Claire was ill at ease and seemed glad to hear Sam was going. "Perhaps so. But thank you for coming by and paying call on Julia. And forgive me for my nosiness, but I must ask: are you two planning to grace the town dance with your presence?"

Sam looked at Julia as he said, "I think we are, ma'am. So is my understanding, anyway."

Julia's smile was but a flicker. "Of course we are," she said.

"Are you two sure there is nothing wrong?"

"Not a thing, ma'am. Not a thing. Good day to you, ladies." And Sam Heller was gone, pausing only to retrieve his mule-leg rifle from the downstairs mantelpiece.

Johnny Cross was on the porch of the Cattleman when Sam Heller passed by, still fuming and confused after his time with Julia. Or was it Della Rose? His brain spinning from it all, and just then noticing Johnny Cross, Heller knew he had to make a decision about all this. Whom was he going to choose to believe? Cross or the lady herself?

"Come up here and have some ham and taters with me, Sam," Johnny Cross said.

Sam trotted up the stairs, realizing he was hungry.

The coffee was especially hot and especially good, leading to Cross teasing the waiter, a Mexican young man named Luis, about the restaurant having forgotten to reuse the previous day's grounds for once. "No, Señor Johnny. No forget nada. Just make sure coffee good for you and Señor Sam."

"Well, we don't forget our friends, Luis," Cross replied. "When Sam and me are all rich and grand and famous, we'll make sure we let folks see you with us in public, and maybe even shake your hand right in front of everybody! We could get Four-eyes Perkins to take a picture of it!"

Luis, uncertain as always about how to take Johnny Cross, chuckled and mumbled, "Gracias, señor," then hustled away. As soon as he was in the kitchen he realized he had never taken their order, and so returned.

Both orders were the same: ham, eggs, biscuits, and fried potatoes. Luis kept the coffee mugs refilled and it was several minutes before any real conversation began.

"So, Sam, have you talked any with the pretty one since I told you what Timothy showed me?"

"I have. Even asked her about the whole name business."

"So, what did she have to say for herself?"

"Well, she did what you'd figure. She denied the whole Skinner business. Swore she's Julia

Canton and her daddy was a preacher and the whole thing just like she said before."

Cross shook his head and took another forkful of potato. "I saw the picture, Sam. She's handing you a bill of goods on that one."

"Know what, Johnny boy? I've just flat-out decided to believe her. She tells me she's who she says, says that picture you say ain't her, and I'm just going to go with what she's saying, till something forces me to do otherwise."

"Faithful as an old hound, are you, Sam?"

"I hope so. I don't see it as a bad way to be."

"Don't know. Sometimes old hounds take some pretty stout kicks."

CHAPTER TWENTY-THREE

Odd feeling in the atmosphere, it seemed to Sam Heller on the morning of the day that would conclude with the huge town dance in and around the big barn just south of Hangtree. He studied the sky, looking for evidence of coming bad weather. He saw nothing.

He had an active day ahead of him, though not of the sort he was accustomed to. He was going to be in the center of the town's attention that evening, and a man needed a good suit for such as that.

There was only one tailor in town, a Scottish man named McCardle who had a shop of sorts framed off in one back corner of the Lockhart Emporium. In some unusual stroke of foresight, Sam had gone to humpbacked old McCardle three weeks earlier and been measured head to toe, an exercise that had required the short Scot to stand on a stool to complete the job. Sam had placed an order for a good black suit, one he could use for occasions ranging from weddings to funerals . . . the only kinds of ceremonies he was prone to be part of. McCardle had notified him a week prior that the suit was ready and waiting, but not until this day had Heller felt any rush to pick it up. He now worried that the blasted thing might not fit, that McCardle could have wrongly measured, considering all the leaning and stretching and squatting he'd had to do just to get all the relevant numbers scribbled down on his little tailor's pad. Beside McCardle, Sam Heller was Goliath.

After a breakfast in a small new eatery that had opened on Mace Street and was struggling valiantly against the well-established Cattleman, Heller strolled through town, thinking again about the questions surrounding Julia Canton. He'd told himself he would take a leap of faith and believe her. Even so, he knew that Johnny Cross, sometime-antagonist and annoyance though he could be, was not a fool. If he swore that the face he'd seen in the Skinner family portrait was Julia's, it wasn't something to be cavalierly dismissed.

Maybe it was time to go to Otto Perkins, and while giving as much protection to Timothy Holt as possible, tell him he'd heard about the Skinner image, and ask to see it for himself. He almost turned his steps toward Perkins's place of business, then reconsidered. Tonight he would be stepping out before his fellow citizens, Julia at his side, bandaged head and all. For this night it was best to let things stand, to let Julia Pepperday Canton be Julia Pepperday Canton, and Della Rose Skinner a nonentity. Get through this one night, reevaluate later, and move on from there and then. Not here and now.

One more night. And it could be a good one . . . especially if he gave Julia no reason to be unhappy with him. She could make it a fine night indeed.

He went on to the Emporium, and there saw Timothy at work on the boardwalk. Heller had momentarily forgotten that the young man had retained his old job with Lockhart even after adding the new one with Perkins. Hard-working fellow, no question of it.

Heller stepped onto the boardwalk and Timothy looked up at him and seemed startled, or in some manner taken aback. "Mr. Sam!" he said. "Hello."

"Hello back atcha."

"Are you here for your suit? It's hanging up back in the tailor corner. Mr. McCardle did a good job on it, like he always does."

"He's good at his work, like you are. In fact, I've wondered how he manages to survive in a town like this, where there's not a lot of demand for tailored clothes."

"He does some work with Mrs. Bewley at the dress shop, too. He makes dresses for her a lot, as an extra job. Kind of like me sweeping for Mr. Otto and also still working here."

"You do what you got to do," Heller said, putting

a foot on the bottom step leading up to the entrance.

Timothy had lost his earlier burst of nervousness and was his usual slightly intense, naturally friendly self. "Let me tell you something: I think Mrs. Bewley sometimes claims that she is the one making the dresses that Mr. McCardle is really making."

"My! Imagine it!"

"Telling lies, Mr. Sam. Lies. And that's bad."

"Yes, I guess it is."

"Have you seen that new dress Miss Julia is wearing to the dance tonight? Really pretty, kind of violet color."

"Haven't seen it. I guess I will tonight."

"Well, every woman who came through the Emporium while Mr. McCardle was working on it stopped and went on about how wonderful it was, and asking who it was for, and all that, like women do."

Heller grinned. "They do talk, that's a fact."

"Well . . ." And here Timothy paused and sidled closer to Heller, speaking in the whispers of a man giving state secrets to an enemy nation. ". . . Mr. McCardle made that dress, and I heard that Mrs. Bewley says she did it!"

"Just plain wicked, Tim, don't you think? But please don't let Mrs. Bewley know I said that."

"I won't. I won't. There's things I'd like to tell you, Mr. Sam, but I ain't free to do it. Things folks said for me to keep secret."

"And you keep secrets when you're asked to, right?"

"That's right, that's right."

"Good man, Timothy. But I do want to ask you if there are any secrets you're keeping that you might personally think I need to know about?"

"Like what, sir?"

"I don't know. Like maybe if somebody is planning to steal some of my cattle. Or maybe anything about my good lady friend, Miss Julia."

"Why are you asking about her?"

"Tell you the truth, Tim, I've begun to notice things that make me wonder if she's telling me, and all of us, the truth about herself. Who she is and so on."

Timothy gaped, clearly having much he wished to say, but fighting himself over whether to say it.

"Because, Timothy, I think she might be named something different. Della, maybe."

Timothy looked scared now. Had he somehow let the information out without knowing it? Yet he thought it right that Mr. Sam, being as close as he was to Julia, should know what there was to be known. He made a decision, praying that it was the right one.

"I ain't supposed to say, but there's a picture Mr. Otto has, shows Black Ear Skinner's family years back. One of the people in it is Miss Julia, younger than now. But it's her. Mr. Otto sees it that way—and he was the one who made the picture, so he saw her in real life—and Mr. Cro—somebody else who looked at it thought it was her, too. But if it is, that means her real name is Della Rose Skinner, and her papa was a bad, bad outlaw."

"It may be true, Tim. But we don't know for sure, and until we do we need to not call anyone a liar. Don't you agree?"

"I do, Mr. Sam."

"I'm going in to see if my suit fits now. You're doing a good job out here, Tim. You'll be at the dance tonight?"

"Yes. But I won't have a lady with me. The one I wanted to go with is going with . . . you."

"Who knows, Tim? She might have taken the worse end of that bargain. I got a feeling you'd treat a young lady right."

"I'd sure try, Mr. Sam. I'd try real hard."

"Talk to you later, Timothy."

"Sir."

Heller went inside.

On most days, banker Arvil Caldwell went home for his lunch. It was an easy, brisk walk and a pleasant dose of fresh air after the enclosed staleness of the Hangtree Bank.

Typically, he either found the house empty, meaning Bridgette and Angeline were out at the little makeshift schoolhouse that stood behind the Hangtree Church. The meager little place actually belonged to the church trustees, and the school was substantially an unofficial and unaffiliated entity, possessing no real schoolmaster or schoolmarm. The mothers, and occasionally,

fathers, of the handful of children who attended
Pecos Academy School provided the teaching
and leadership on their own, coming together
for the benefit of sharing the work involved and
giving the children a chance to know and play
with one another. Angeline was fairly new to the
Academy, young as she was, but she loved it and
Caldwell was happy she had the opportunity to
be part of it.

He did not anticipate his two ladies would be
absent today, though. This was a "home study" day
for the informal school, so he expected to find
wife and daughter with their noses buried in a
book, working hard.

"Bridgette? I'm here!"

The house was strangely silent, and felt empty
as he entered the rear door. "Angeline, honey?
Are you here? Where is Mama?"

No reply. Caldwell's heart began to pound
harder. This was not right. Something was
wrong . . . he could feel it.

A moment's pause reminded him that they
might be merely out on a walk, or visiting the
outhouse, or the garden, or a neighbor . . . there
was certainly no evidence of anything to panic
over.

Forcing himself to calm down, he went for a
crockery vessel in which he knew there were cold
biscuits from the morning, and probably two or
three well-fried sausages. An entirely sufficient
lunch.

The food was there but he found it tasteless
and ate only half a biscuit and sausage before

putting it aside. He couldn't shake off the sense of something being amiss. He began to explore the house, quietly calling for his wife and daughter.

He found nothing to disturb him except their absence. Until he climbed the stairs and neared an unused rear room with wall access to an attic storage room. When he walked into the rear room, heels clunking, he thought he heard a small, tremoring voice that at first he thought was a bird trapped in the adjacent attic. Then he thought it sounded like the soft vocal noises little Angelina sometimes made when she napped in the big overstuffed chair downstairs. He went to the closed access door to the attic space and leaned close to it.

"Angelina? Are you in there?"

This time a reply, clearly spoken. "Arvil!"

It was not Angelina, but Bridgette. He found his wife bound and lying on the floor inside the attic space, her wrists raw from her efforts to free herself and her feet swollen below the area where over-tight restraints had been tied just above her ankles. Her face streamed with tears and a gag she had managed to work loose with teeth and tongue hung damp around her neck. Her hands were tied behind her back, with a rope leading down to join with the one binding her ankles.

"God, honey! Oh God, dear, tell me, what happened? Are you hurt? Where is Angelina?"

"He took her . . . he took her, Arvil!"

"Are you hurt?"

"No. Just sore and stiff from being tied here all morning."

"Who was this man and where did he take our daughter?" So many dreadful possibilities were flooding Caldwell's mind that he was near to bursting into tears. Bridgette's streaked and reddened face revealed she had done plenty of crying of her own already.

"Who was he?"

"A stranger. Nothing unusual about him . . . he was friendly, and talked so sweetly to Angeline when he came to the door. She heard him knock and was closer to the door than I was . . . I was dragging that big tin washtub out of that back closet and didn't even hear the knock. She shouldn't have done it, but she opened the door and let him in.

"When I came back in the room and saw him standing there near Angeline, I think I might have yelled. I jumped back hard enough to trip myself and sprawled out on my rump. He came over, looking very concerned, and put his hand out to help me up. I wouldn't take it, wouldn't touch him without knowing who he was and why he was here. I got up on my own and went over to Angeline and put my arm over her. She asked me what was wrong, and told me her 'new friend' was Uncle Cale, and that he was a friend of yours."

"I've never known a 'Cale' in my life, and certainly I have no uncle or relation by that name."

"I'd never heard you mention such a name, so that made me mistrust this man even more. And then . . . he asked me if I might spare him a bite to eat, and I realized this was probably just some drifter who went door-to-door to find his meals. He was certainly no fat man, but he wasn't too thin, either, so he gets something to eat from somewhere. I made him a sandwich with the last of the cheese and those store-bought pickles you brought back from San Antonio. He thanked me and ate. I thought he would leave then, but instead he reached in a pocket and pulled out a little pistol—what do they call those little, frilly-looking ones? Derringers?—it was one of those. He had the friendliest grin on his face, but he held that derringer up and aimed it right at Angeline. My breath went away and for a long while, probably near two minutes, I couldn't breathe at all, no matter how hard I tried.

"Angeline, she thought that derringer was a toy, I think, and that he was offering it to her, because she reached out for it. He lost his smile all at once and sort of snarled at her, enough to make her move back. He says to her, 'Know what that is, darling? That's a little girl dead-maker. It kills little girls just as dead as stones in the creek.' I shuddered to hear it, and I think most of it went right past Angeline because she just looked solemn and confused, and maybe like she wondered if she'd done something wrong."

"Dear God above!" Arvil Caldwell declared in a hoarse whisper. "What did this devil want?"

"I think, Arvil . . . I think he wants *you*. He told me to tell you that he and Angeline will be waiting for you at the bank tomorrow morning at seven. He says come alone, and not to tell a soul about any of this, especially the law." She paused and began to cry. "He said if he gets even a sniff of law or other interference in the morning, the first thing that happens is that Angeline dies. And he'll do it, too, Arvil. I could tell he's the kind who would really do it."

"God, Bridgette, I think he's robbing the bank! He wants me in there to get him into the vault!"

"Arvil, you aren't going to tell the law, are you? Please don't do it, if you're thinking that. He'll kill her, he will! I think he might have killed me before he left except he wanted me to be able to tell you all this without him having to write it down."

Arvil Caldwell realized he was quaking from head to toe, as much as if he were outdoors in a bitter winter far, far to the north. He saw his little girl's face with every blink of his eye and in every corner into which he turned his gaze.

What was he going to do? He needed help, but was forbidden from seeking it. And the price of disobedience would be the life of his little girl. His own beloved little girl.

CHAPTER TWENTY-FOUR

There would be no surprises come evening when Claude Farley revealed his new waltz composed in honor of Julia because he spent most of the day practicing it outdoors. By midafternoon most of Hangtree's residents had heard the tune at least three times. Claude could take comfort, though, in the general consensus that he'd done a good job of composing.

Timothy Holt had actually adapted his sweeping to three-quarter time, brushing along while he hummed the tune he'd heard drifting over the breeze much of the day. He was reaching the part he liked best when a carriage passed, raising dust and annoying him because it undid much of his best cleaning. He glanced up to see who the driver was. It was a man he didn't recognize, a stranger to Hangtree. But for only a moment, he thought he saw young Angeline Caldwell peep around the raised carriage hood. The man, he figured, must be a relative or family friend, because he saw neither of Angeline's parents.

To Timothy's surprise, the driver rolled the carriage to a stop before the Emporium and waved for Timothy to come over. He did, and found that it was indeed Angeline Caldwell in the vehicle with the stranger. She looked nervous to him, and was sitting back squarely against the seat, as if trying to stay as out-of-view as possible. Timothy wondered if the man had told her to do that.

"Hello, Angeline," Timothy said, smiling. "Where are your mother and father?"

The little girl looked like she wanted to answer, but the man with her glared over at her, and then turned a happier expression to Timothy. "She is with her uncle Cale this morning. We are having a very pleasant ride. But I didn't call you over here to tell you that. You know Angeline, I can see . . . do you know many others in this town?"

"I get to know most everybody because of my job here at the Emporium," Timothy replied. "Everybody goes up and down these steps and across this walk, and they see me."

"Might you know a very pretty young lady who has come lately and calls herself Julia Canton?"

"Yes, yes, I know Miss Julia."

"I need you to deliver her a message for me," the man said. "Can you do that? I'll give you two whole dollars in advance if you'll get the job done."

"Yes, sir. Yes, I can do it."

On the spot, Timothy got his two dollars, which he clutched and then pocketed. Happy as he was for the money, it didn't erase a sense of doubt about this stranger. He instinctively found the man impossible to trust, or to feel positively toward. And the overly friendly smile only heightened the impression of falseness that came from him.

"What do you want me to tell her?" Timothy asked.

The man leaned down. "Listen closely, boy: Tell her that Uncle Cale says she need not be involved in the plan now. We've found a way to move it along without her. The other way we'd talked about. Did you get it?"

"Yes, sir. What does it mean, though?"

"She'll know. You don't need to. You just need to say it right. Now, say it back to me."

Timothy repeated the words almost perfectly, and what minor differences there might have been had no effect on the meaning. Cale Pepperday had him repeat it a third and fourth time before he told Timothy to get the message to her as quickly as possible, and to no one else. And to be sure to remember it came from Uncle Cale.

"So are you uncle to Angeline and to Miss Julia both?"

"Boy, first off, don't ask questions that ain't none of your business. It'll keep you out of a lot of trouble. Second, I'm everybody's uncle. I'm one of those nice gents everybody wants to be their friend and their kin."

"That's good . . . Uncle Cale."

The man shook his head, still holding his smile. "Uh-uh, boy. Your uncle I ain't. I've already been uncle to one half-wit. I don't need another one coming along."

"Uncle Cale" turned his eyes forward and prepared to move the carriage out. In that moment Angeline looked at Timothy with eyes that reflected sadness, questioning, and most of all, fear. He tried to make his own eyes speak back, telling her that whatever was scaring her was going to turn out all right.

He repeated several times to himself the message the man had paid him to deliver. He would get it done, either by speaking to her on the street if he saw her out taking one of her nearly daily walks, or at the big town celebration in the evening. He again repeated to himself what he'd been told to say, and decided to repeat it throughout the day until he finally got it delivered.

He went back to his work with his mind continually turning back to little Angeline and the disturbing man she was with. Probably the man really was her uncle and it was perfectly fine she was with him . . . yet it didn't feel right.

As a couple of hours passed, Timothy's anxiety only heightened, and he decided to go visit the Hangtree Bank and tell Mr. Caldwell he'd seen Angeline, so that Mr. Caldwell could assure him that all was well and she was supposed to be with that man, her uncle Cale. He was tired of worrying.

Getting permission to leave early from the storekeeper Lockhart, Timothy made his way to the Hangtree Bank and slipped in. A cluster of people were gathered in a corner, backs to Timothy, speaking to someone their forms hid from him. Timothy was curious, but he was here to find Caldwell.

Caldwell seemingly was not there. His office door was open but no one was present. Timothy asked Wilson, a teller, if he knew where Caldwell was, and got a shrug in reply. "He was here this morning," Wilson, a gruff-voiced man, said. "Ain't come back since he went home for lunch." Wilson edged a little closer. "Know what I think? Got him that pretty wife at home, and . . ." Wilson made a circle with the thumb and forefinger of his left hand, and pushed his right-hand index finger up through it, grinning in a way Timothy didn't like. "Know what I'm telling you, boy?"

Timothy didn't, but pretended he did. He pondered that bank teller Wilson gave him a bad feeling something like the one "Uncle Cale" in the carriage had roused.

Timothy turned to go. Just then the little crowd in the corner broke up, and the person who had been holding their attention emerged from among them. It was Julia Canton.

She noticed Timothy and smiled, coming his way. "Hello, my good friend! What a happy surprise to see you!" She patted his arm and leaned up to whisper. "Walk me out of here, would you? I've been surrounded by people in here and I need some fresh air."

Since her refusal to go to the upcoming dance

with him, Timothy had viewed Julia in a cloud of negative uncertainty, particularly since he'd seen that picture of young Della Rose Skinner in Mr. Otto's big book of photographs. Much of that cloud was instantly pierced through and dissipated. He welcomed the fact that she seemed to welcome him.

She even tucked her arm around his and let him escort her out just as if he was . . . somebody. Timothy rarely felt like a somebody. Yet here he was, marching out of the bank in front of all Hangtree, his arm held by the prettiest and momentarily most-celebrated person in town.

Walking tall and straight like his mother encouraged him to do, Timothy kept glancing at the bandage on Julia's brow. "How's your head feeling, Miss Julia?" he asked.

"I'm healing up well, Timothy, thank you. The pain is mostly gone, though I still have a headache in the mornings when I sit up. Especially if I sit up too quickly, or bump my head on anything. Bumping my head is the worst of it now."

"I hope it don't leave no scar, ma'am. 'Cause I always thought you had a pretty forehead."

She chuckled. "I've never been specifically complimented on my forehead before, Timothy. It's quite nice. And I'm very hopeful there'll be no scar, or at least not much of one."

"I'm glad."

"And what about you, Timothy? How are you doing?"

The question brought back all his concerns in

a rush. He slumped a little. "I'm worried, ma'am. About a little girl in town here. I was in the bank just now hoping to see her daddy, 'cause he works there. But he ain't there this afternoon. Hey, why were all them people around you in there?"

A wry expression crossed Julia's face. "People are odd ducks, Timothy. They're always looking for somebody to watch and hold up on their shoulders or stand on a pedestal, because those people are stronger or bigger or braver or prettier or whatever. Well, for some reason this town has decided to make me that person. Until the next one comes along."

"I don't understand."

"Have you heard the story about how I stopped that man from robbing the church folk on a Sunday morning? Well, people thought about that story awhile and decided it meant I was the great heroine of Hangtree. Simple Georgia girl brings down the bad man with nothing but a church offering plate. That kind of thing."

"It was mighty brave of you, Miss Julia."

"I doubt 'brave' is exactly the right word. If something had gone wrong and he'd shot somebody that Sunday morning, people would be cursing my name instead of praising me and gathering around me in a bank lobby just so they can tell people they talked to me and 'know' me. There's a thin line between heroism and foolishness, Tim. Very thin. It all comes down to the choices made and whether they turn out for good or bad."

"I think I know what you mean. Can I ask you another question?"

"Certainly."

"How can you tell a good man from a bad one? Can you tell just from looking at him or talking to him?"

"I don't think so. People are good or bad based on what they do. And maybe what they think, and how they think. A plain or even ugly person or even one it is hard to like—or even a simple person—can be a good person. And someone can be handsome, or strong, or pretty and lady-like, and be a very bad person in the things they do and the things they think." She stopped, thoughtful and frowning as much as her injured and bandaged brow would allow.

"Is something wrong?"

She squeezed Timothy's arm with her own. "No. You just made me think about some things, that's all."

"Can I ask you one more question?"

"Go ahead. But remember, my answers may not be the best ones you can find. I'm just a lady, not Socrates."

"Who?"

"Never mind. What's the question?"

"Do you have an uncle whose name is Cale?"

She yanked her arm from his and got directly in front of him, gazing unblinking into his face and making him redden and seem to shrink in stature a few inches. "Why do you ask me that, Tim? Have you met this 'Uncle Cale'?"

Timothy often didn't know the right thing to do, but this time he did. He made himself look at her probing, glaring eyes, and said, "Can we find a place to sit down in the shade somewhere? I want to tell you something."

She located a shaded alley beside a small carpentry shop, and sat down on an old thrown-out nail keg. Timothy remained afoot and paced back and forth as he talked.

He told her about the Caldwell family, parents and child, and about his experience with the carriage, and Angeline's pleading look, and the odd and unsettling man who had given him a message to deliver to Julia. And of his sense that Angeline was not really supposed to be with that man.

"What was the message?" Julia asked.

Timothy's mind had been so busy the last little while that he panicked for a moment and forgot what he'd memorized and repeated to himself most of the day.

But it returned quickly. "Uncle Cale says she—that means you, Miss Julia—need not be involved in the plan now. They've found a way to move it along without you. The other way they'd talked about. That was what he said to tell you. He said you'd know what it meant."

"I'm afraid I do. And he had this little girl with him as he said all this?"

"Yes. Right there beside him. I don't think she wanted to be there."

"Timothy, we have to go to that girl's parents right now. Can you take me to where the Caldwells live?"

CHAPTER TWENTY-FIVE

With the Caldwells both in tears and clinging to one another while Julia spoke softly but terrifyingly of the man who had taken their daughter, Timothy sat tensely in a corner of their parlor, eyes on a door he wished he could bolt out of and find an ordinary world beyond. He despised sadness and fear, having known plenty of both in his life, and it tormented him to see the Caldwells, good people, going through so much of both right now.

"I wish I'd just grabbed her out of the carriage," he murmured, looking down between his feet.

"What?" Julia asked, pausing in her talk.

"Nothing. Nothing. Just thinking."

"Oh God, what might he do with her?" asked Bridgette Caldwell, her voice choked and quaking.

"If you cooperate, nothing, or so I hope," Julia said. She'd already admitted to two humiliating things: to her actual blood relationship with Cale

Pepperday, her late mother's brother, and to her involvement in a conspiracy to rob a bank, particularly to doing some of the initial research to find a particularly vulnerable but richly deposited bank at a location far enough away from much anywhere to draw ready notice. She confessed to having helped develop the specifics of the robbery plan: stampeding a huge herd of cattle through a cow town in as damaging and dangerous a way as possible, thereby creating such an overwhelming distraction that whatever law enforcement there was would have little chance to notice, much less react to, a bank robbery. It sounded like a mad scheme, she admitted, but told the story of the partially similar incident farther east, and declared that it was the very wildness of the scheme that made it likely to work. No one would anticipate such a thing.

What she didn't reveal was anything related to the name Skinner. Nothing about the fact that she was herself Skinner's offspring, or that the conspirators behind the scheme were, to a man, old members of the Black Ear gang. None of that was relevant to the only real concern at hand: getting back young Angeline safe and sound.

"Beyond the things that are obvious from what he's done, what can you tell us about this Pepperday fellow who has done this to us?" Arvil Caldwell asked. "Has he ever kidnapped or harmed a child before?"

"No," Julia was glad to reply. Her words became, from that point, true but deliberately vague. "My uncle Cale is a man who entered crime because of opportunity, not through an inherent criminal nature. He was placed in a situation of coming to know an active outlaw through the marriage of one of his relatives, and that outlaw tempted him to join his gang with promises of easy wealth, freedom, and fame with the kind of people who admire outlaws. He joined in, and it changed him, slowly, from a decent, normal man at the start to a criminal-minded man later on. Until he visited me this week to tell me about the death of my mother, I hadn't seen him in years. What I'm telling you is, I don't know what he might do, because I don't know how far down the slope he's progressed since I've really known him last."

"He might kill her, oh, dear, sweet Jesus, no!" Bridgette's voice was growing higher and more tremulous. "Oh, merciful Jesus, protect our child!"

Arvil put his arms around his wife more firmly, and they wept together. Timothy wanted to weep, too, and also to get away from all this overwhelming sorrow.

Tears in her own eyes, Julia tried to sound as reassuring as she could. "He might . . . or he might not. But I can tell you this: I am fully confident that if you are cooperative, he will not hurt her, and will return her to you safely. But you must take him seriously when he warns you against turning to the law, or any other such entity, to protect her. I know too little about him as he is now, that's true. But I know enough of some of the men around him to know that they would not hesitate to do dreadful harm to her, even to kill her. You must not, *must* not, speak to any officer of the law about this."

Arvil found the strength to look Julia in the eye. "Pardon me, ma'am, but why should we trust the word of someone who has just confessed to her involvement to the very conspiracy that had put our child, not to mention my employing bank and the town at large, into danger?"

"I can . . . I can hardly find an answer to that. There is little evidence I can present in my own favor. Just know this: I might have enough greed and potential criminality in my soul to allow me to take money from a bank. I do not possess sufficient darkness of spirit to allow me to see a child hurt or killed simply to clear the path for me to gain good fortune. I didn't have to come to you today to tell you any of this, but I did so, of my own choice. Take that into account as you pass judgment on me."

He stared at her darkly. "Account taken."

"Here is what tallies on the bottom line of the ledger for me: I was willing to help with the planning of the bank robbery using stampeding cattle as a cover. As soon as talk turned to a second, alternate plan, one involving the taking of a hostage related to someone at the bank in order to force that person's cooperation, at that point I withdrew my cooperation. I would play whatever part I could in the first formulation of the plan, but in no way would I take part in anything that might lead to the murder of an innocent. I did not help plan that version of the scheme, but I heard it planned. That was what my uncle was telling me . . . that the second plan, the one I declined to take part in, was the one they were moving to."

"Just tell us what we should do in order to save our girl," pleaded Bridgette.

"He told you, Mr. Caldwell, to be at the bank at seven tomorrow morning?"

"He told me that through Bridgette. I've not spoken to him myself."

"All the same, follow his instruction. Exactly. Resist any temptation to notify authorities. Your daughter's life may depend on it."

"He'll want me to open the vault."

"He will. And you must do it. And give him access to any other items he may ask for."

"I will do just that. I don't like being party to the robbery of a bank that has been good to me, a second home to me, really . . . but my daughter's safety is all that matters. Whatever happens to me after that, so be it."

"That is precisely the attitude you must have, Mr. Caldwell. Bring Angeline home, first and foremost, then after that, and only after that, address any other issues that arise out of it all."

"Such as my loss of employment."

"That's a likely result, yes. But again, it's the safety of Angeline that matters."

Bridgette was watching Julia closely. "Are you certain you are not part of this conspiracy even now? I am sorry to ask you that, but it strikes me that all you've done is tell us to cooperate with these evil people, which it seems to me serves *their* purposes as much as ours."

"But your purpose, the life of your child, is of such high importance that all other concerns vanish."

"Yes. But I have to know something: are you going to gain from the proceeds of this robbery, if it happens?"

"I would have done so, but not now. Not that a child has been put in danger as part of the scheme. I'm not a woman of the highest scruples in all areas of my life, but that I will not take part in, nor profit from."

"I suppose we simply have to trust you on that, as on everything else you've said."

"Yes. I suppose you must."

"I've got to go to the outhouse," announced Timothy. "Real bad. Can I?"

"Go on, Tim," said Arvil. "You know where it is. But hurry out . . . thinking about this situation, I may have to go in there soon to vomit."

Timothy soon vacated the outhouse, but opted to stay out in the fresh air rather than wade back into the murk of tension inside the house. So when Arvil replaced Tim in the outhouse, the women were left alone a few moments.

Bridgette, managing for a few moments to keep better control of her emotions, managed a very weak and faltering smile for perhaps two seconds. "I want to tell you, Miss Canton, I do appreciate you coming to us to try to help." The last of the smile died. "But I also despise you for ever being part of a plan that brought such bad men to this place. What you did laid the groundwork for my little girl being taken away from me. If you and your conspirators hadn't come up with this evil scheme of yours, my little girl would be sitting beside me right now, us reading together, maybe singing a song. She likes to sing with me. But because of what you and your people started, I may never sing with her again." She paused and squeezed her eyes shut, new tears streaming. After a moment or two she managed to go on. "And do you know what is happening tonight in this town? They are dedicating that big town dance to you, honoring you, because they like what you did to that thief in the church when he tried to rob everyone. And they think it's wonderful that you killed the man who tried to misuse you. They say you are a heroine of Hangtree, and they are going to play music for you and give you a piece of stone with your name chiseled on it, and calling you a 'heroine.' You aren't supposed to know about it, but now I've told you. You are no heroine. You are good for coming to us and trying to help us today, but if not for what you've done, we would not need help at all."

"You're right, Mrs. Caldwell. But I can't change what has already happened. So what is it you want me to say? What do you want me to do?"

"I want you to say that you will not accept whatever honor they try to give you tonight. I want you to stand before the town and say you are a criminal and do not deserve to be honored. I want you to do that tonight."

Julia felt shaken, deeply. She had again a sense of being a train about to jump its track. She didn't know what to think of what Bridgette Caldwell was saying to her, or what her response should be. When she opened her mouth and began to speak, it was as if she were hearing it said by someone else.

And she also knew she had said just the right thing. She cared not at all about being honored by the town. But neither could she allow a situation this precarious to be guided by the overwrought emotions of a terrified mother.

"Mrs. Caldwell, please think about what you're saying. The men who are going to rob the bank are camped outside town already. They've been gathering up a herd, a huge one, for weeks now. And they've got your daughter. We don't know how closely or for how long they may have been watching everything going on in Hangtree. They may know all about this honor I'm to be given tonight. If things change suddenly, if I start acting strangely and different from my usual self, they will treat that just the same as if you openly went to the law. And they would kill Angeline."

The distraught mother cried a little more, trembling from head to toe. "You seem very sure of what these animals will or won't do. And it seems that . . . that . . ." She trailed off, unable to find words. But they were provided for her by her husband, who had quietly reentered the house, unnoticed, while Julia was speaking.

"It seems that the interests of Julia Pepperday Canton seem always to line up with the interests of the ones who have our daughter. That's strangely coincidental, isn't it! Could it be that, at the end of all this, Miss Canton is going to enjoy her share of the ill-gotten gain? That maybe this little charitable, helpful visit you've made here is all part of the plan, a way to make sure that unpredictable Mr. and Mrs. Caldwell, the ones who can get that vault door open, dance all the right steps and don't get out of line. Is that what you were trying to say to Miss Canton, dear?"

"Yes. Yes. Exactly."

"I thought so. I had a few moments to think it over out there, and I realized that the kind of woman who would associate with criminals and plan a bank robbery isn't likely to have a sudden conversion and turn into the Mother of Righteousness. You aren't helping us out of some desire to be a good human being and tread the streets of gold someday. You're working for your share of the money."

Julia, trembling herself now, looked the man in the face. "I vow to both of you, I will accept not a cent of any money taken in that bank robbery. And if your daughter dies, I will personally end the life of the man who took her, relation of mine though he may be. I vow it to you!"

Caldwell nodded. "And here's my vow back to you: If my daughter dies, even if you and your vile people get your hands on every cent in that bank, and rob every bank between here and the farthest tip of Maine, and use it to bury yourselves from the rest of the world, know that I will find you. No matter what or no matter how far or long, I will find you. And you will pay the fullest price. That is my vow to you. Believe it. Now go."

With no further words spoken, Julia Canton left the Caldwell house, rejoined Timothy outside, and walked back to the parsonage of the Hangtree Church. The day was going by and it was time to begin to get ready for the evening.

The prettiest woman in Hangtree had a dance to attend with the handsomest man, and the richest, Sam Heller.

CHAPTER TWENTY-SIX

As town dances in Hangtree went, this one would go down in history. The music was better-practiced than usual, Fiddling Claude Farley had a particularly good night, and his original composition for the occasion, "The Brave Maiden Waltz," received applause and hoots and five demands for encore. Claude good-naturedly obliged them all.

Torchlight lit the area outside the horse barn, giving a beautiful golden glow across the dancing people and lighting the rising smoke from the pits where pigs roasted. The delicious smell wafted across the entire area, reaching even to the unseen horsemen who sat in a line in the darkness, pondering whether to send one or two of their number in to gather up a couple of bucketfuls of barbecue, then deciding it was too much of a risk.

Drew Toleen spat tobacco amber onto the ground and said to the rider beside him, "After tomorrow morning, we'll be able to buy all the meat in Texas."

The sound of applause reached the mounted watchers.

"Hey, look at that . . . they've got Della Rose up on the platform, giving her some kind of award. What the hell!"

"She's big and famous and brave now, don't you know? And she ain't Della Rose to those people there. Calls herself Julia Canton now. Uses the middle name of Pepperday."

"Like Cale?"

"Cale's sister was Della's mother. So Pepperday was her maiden name."

"I be damned! Learn something new all the time. Speaking of Cale, he still got that gal locked down good?"

"Locked up, actually . . . she's locked inside an old woodshed left from when there was a settlement there."

"I been thinking . . . why bother with stampeding the cattle? We got the daughter of one of the bankers . . . why not just have him open the vault up for us, get the money, and run our asses out of there?"

"Because you'd not be out of town before some lawman was on us and a posse was after us. Run a big herd of cattle through that town, knocking down a few buildings, trampling a few folks to death, and by the time they know the bank was robbed, we'll be miles away, rich men."

"Hope it all goes right."

"It will. It will. Look there . . . Della Rose is dancing with that big hombre!"

And she was. She and Sam Heller waltzed masterfully to the tune of Claude's new composition while the admiring population of Hangtree looked on. As in her dream, those minutes removed from her all other concerns, worries, even awarenesses. She looked into his face and he looked back at hers, unheeding of the bandage on her brow and the occasional unsteadiness of her feet.

Then the music stopped and the applause renewed. Julia looked around at her admirers and accepted their veneration, but back into her consciousness crept the realization that out in the darkness was a big herd of cattle that in the morning would violently rampage through this town. And in the bank, a young girl would be held at gunpoint until her father helped a criminal gang empty the vault of a bank he was pledged to protect.

The dancing, eating, and drinking went on long after the ceremonial honoring of the "Brave Maiden of Hangtree" was concluded. Though she left the dance ground and retired to one of the chairs circling it, there to enjoy a plate of roasted pig and, she hoped, some quiet conversation with her escort. But she and Heller received almost no opportunity to converse. A stream of well-wishers and congratulators moved past her, each person eager to have his or her moment with the celebrated woman of the hour. Despite a mind filled with worries and distractions, Julia maintained her cordiality throughout. It was not easy.

Nor was it easy to overhear bits of conversation around her: People asking one another where the Caldwell family was. Had they not attended? Bridgette Caldwell was known to be an excellent dancer, and the delightful young Angeline Caldwell showed promise of possessing equivalent skill. It was impossible to imagine what might have kept them from this event.

If only they knew, Julia thought. *Dear God, if only they knew.*

Not a moment of sleep had touched the mind and body of Arvil Caldwell by the time the sky began to lighten the next morning. He was up and shakily making a pot of coffee more than an hour before his early "appointment" at the Hangtree Bank. He'd had time over the sleepless hours to make peace with what he was being forced to do. He was past any sense of guilt over turning over the bank's assets. He felt badly about it, to be sure, but a man with no choice was a man with no choice. He would meet the robbers at seven, open the bank's doors and just as readily open the vault, and even help them load up their takings for removal. Whatever it took to get his daughter back again.

When he thought of how much Sam Heller would be hurt by this, he cringed. Sam was a friend as well as the bank's key depositor. It pained him to think he would see his friend's fortune carried out by scoundrels, and this after Caldwell had spent so much time trying to persuade Heller of the security of his bank.

Amazingly, Bridgette had managed to fall asleep, something her husband put down to the exhaustion brought on by extreme worry. For a time, her husband had lain there beside her, sitting up against the headboard and staring into the darkness, praying and wondering where his child was at that moment, and in what circumstances this night was passing for her. There were no words for the level of distress it caused him.

Caldwell managed to get down one cup of coffee and then could wait no longer. He went to his wife, ready to kiss her and gently awaken her for a good-bye. He couldn't bring himself to do it. What good would it do her to be awake and worrying, when she was powerless to change the situation?

It was Arvil who held that power, and he vowed to himself and the heavens that he would exercise it. He would return with their daughter safe at his side, and never let her face such terror again, whatever it required.

He trudged through the dimmest part of morning toward the bank, making sure he had the required keys, and his written-down listing of the vault combination. He could not risk a failure of memory with so much at stake.

Praying silently, he took the longest walk of his life.

Unknown to him, he was not alone on the streets. Others were awake, two of them a pair of bachelor brothers, generally referred to jointly as "Them Drunken Earhardt Brothers." They had lived up to their collective sobriquet at the previous night's town dance, drinking excessive amounts of cheap beer provided by the Dog Star. One of them, Aaron, had followed his usual habit of out-guzzling his brother, and naturally had been the first to pass out, hugging the back of an outhouse near the farrier shop. His brother, Austin, drank more slowly and managed to avoid passing out at all, but he did stretch out on the ground a few yards away from his brother to sleep out the night. He awakened first as well, and stirred his brother back to life. They stumbled along together now, up through town, blocked by their location from any view of the shadowy moving figure of Arvil Caldwell.

The Earhardts were seen, though, but not by Caldwell. Their halting progress was tracked by the eyes of Pedro Sanchez, who worked in the kitchen of the Cattleman and was dumping a batch of old grease into a pit behind the building, much to the interest of a pack of semi-feral dogs whose home was the streets. The Mexican, who had fought and won his own battle with alcohol, watched them and said a quick prayer for them, genuflecting as he did so.

Also seeing them was Julia Canton, up early after failing to sleep for much the same reason as Arvil Caldwell. She had no intention of being at the bank when the Black Ear gunnies showed up, but she did hope to see Angeline safely returned to her father and to find a good vantage point from which to watch the anticipated stampede.

Clad in a ragged old dress rather than the fine lavender-colored one she had worn the night before, she was also wearing her plainest and most serviceable old shoes, tie-ups worthy of an old maid schoolmarm. There was a reason for her rugged garb. She had an idea of where she wanted to be when the cattle surged into the street: a balcony attached the to same building housing the local farrier. The rooms behind it were unused and empty. To get to the balcony from the outside, she would have to climb.

She reached the spot and realized that she also would have a good view of the bank from the balcony—another plus. Taking a quick look around to make sure she was not being watched, she darted to a trestle running up one side of the balcony-topped porch, and clambered up it fast, especially so for a lady who had recently suffered a major concussive injury. On the balcony, she noticed a filthy old rug that had been hung over the railing. Good cover to remain behind so as to see without being seen in turn.

She got in place and began to watch the bank. No lights burned there yet, but it seemed to her a shadow moved behind one of the windows. Someone was already inside. Caldwell, probably.

She settled and from a large and specially made pocket on the side of her dress removed a pistol. She examined it, making sure it was loaded. She had no special plan to use it, but this was a dangerous enterprise and she felt better with some means of protecting herself.

Tired and hurting from a night spent tied up on a woodshed floor, Angeline Caldwell was sure she was on the way to her death. Though the man who called himself Uncle Cale made token efforts to be kindly, he had an underlying manner that gave the lie to it. At her young age and coming from a close and loving family, Angeline knew far more of good than of bad, so it was hard for her to realize that what she was feeling in the person of Cale Pepperday was simply a great depth of evil.

She was behind him on the saddle, riding double with her arms around him as if he really were her uncle and someone she was happy to be with. It was only threats, though, that kept her clinging to the man. He had told her that if he felt her let go of him, he would cut her arms off at the elbows and see how she liked *that*. She clung on hard.

They shunned the main street and approached the bank from the side and rear. Cale and his prisoner girl, three others of the gang, and that was all. The others were all delegated to start, and as much as possible, direct the coming huge stampede. Once the first wave of cattle tore onto the streets, the others would follow the same path. It was going to be something to see, and dangerous to be part of. The biggest crowd of living creatures Hangtree had ever seen. But the payoff, oh, that would be worth every risk.

The rear door of the bank was open, as planned, and they entered to find Caldwell waiting for them in the most open part of the lobby. His arms were raised on each side of him to shoulder level. His eyes darted quickly over every man entering, looking for his daughter.

And there she was, coming in ahead of a man he somehow knew at once had to be the "Uncle Cale" who had brought such terror to his wife, and stolen his daughter. Cale Pepperday had a pistol raised and pressed between the child's shoulder blades, and she was shaking hard, and clearly fighting not to cry.

That battle was lost the moment she saw her father. "Daddy!" she exclaimed, and started to bolt to him, but Cale Pepperday's hand shot out and caught her by her clothing. "Not yet, pretty one, not yet," he said. "Daddy's got some work to do for us before you go back to him. He's helping us out, like a good little bank monkey. Ain't that right, bank monkey? Lending a hand to good old Uncle Cale and his friends? Have you got the vault open for us, monkey boy?"

"It's open," Caldwell said as firmly as he could. It was hard to speak at all just now.

"Get in there and show your new friends here where the big money is. And any diamonds tucked away in there by your local biddies, or any gold and silver and such. We want to carry as much out of this place as we can, and we intend for what we carry to be worth the burden. No dollar notes or half-dimes or pennies or any such as that. Now move."

Caldwell had been counting on being brought into the vault, because it provided him an opportunity these thieves had no way of knowing about, an opportunity that, once remembered, had filled him with fantasies of violent rescue of his daughter, thwarting of the robbery, and simultaneous lethal punishment of the robbers.

Now that they were actually present, and Angeline was in the midst of it all and potentially in the line of any fire that might break out, the fantasy seemed much less plausible. Especially when Pepperday ordered one of his associates to keep guard over Angeline so that she would not attempt to flee prematurely.

"You done good so far, banker man," said Pepperday as he and Caldwell entered the vault, which was the size of a small room and lined with stout shelves. On some of those shelves were small double-lock strongboxes containing cash, jewels, precious metals, and other items of value. Each strongbox belonged to a customer of the bank, and Caldwell possessed only one of the keys needed to open the boxes, the others being in possession of the individual customers. If these thieves wanted to get at the contents of the small boxes, they would have to carry the strongboxes out complete and break into them elsewhere, and later.

"Listen!" Pepperday said sharply and suddenly, raising his hand.

Caldwell did, then said, "I don't hear—" and cut off fast, because he did hear it, felt it, actually, more than heard. A distant, advancing rumble, not much different from muffled thunder from a long way off.

It had started. And as the thieves in the still-darkened bank began to detect it, a cheer rose from them, kept low, but still a cheer. Hands slapped together in celebration . . .

. . . and attention was diverted for a few moments. Moments that Angeline Caldwell took advantage of to dart out the same door through which they had entered, the man assigned to watch her having become distracted by the approach of the stampeding cattle.

CHAPTER TWENTY-SEVEN

Like many in Hangtree that morning, Otto Perkins was awakened by the feeling of something like an earthquake. In the back room of his makeshift studio and shop, he sat up in his bed, confused and wondering whether the poorly made building enclosing him would stand up. When he felt a tremendous jolt and heard a nearly explosive slamming noise at the front of the building facing the street, he was convinced he was about to be buried in falling lumber.

The rumbling and shaking continued, but the room stayed intact around him. Perkins rose and slid the half-circle grips of his eyeglasses around his ears, and rose with trepidation.

Out the front window of his building he saw an amazing sight: waves of bovine flesh and the flashing broad expanses of wide cattle horns, tossing and tilting as they moved. He noticed his front porch was knocked nearly loose from the building; the falling of part of the porch roof and two of the supports accounted for the jolt and slamming noise he'd heard. He felt and heard the building creak, and yelled in surprise when a side window exploded inward and a young bullock burst through, having been driven against the building by the pressure of the herd. The window frame and some of the wall splintered apart as the entire young bull came inside. Perkins backed up and clambered fast onto the shop counter and stood there cringing, the heels of his hands pressed to his whimpering mouth. He looked like a sissified schoolmaster terrified by a rat on the classroom floor. The bullock, eyes wild and glaring from the animal emotion of the stampede, burst its way out the double front doors, across the porch, and back into the surge.

Only then did Perkins notice that the stampede did not appear to be a totally natural one. Occasionally a rider would pass on the side of the thundering herd, whooping and waving a hat and seemingly trying to avoid having the cattle turn down side streets and alleys.

It struck Perkins that this was the most exciting event he'd seen in his life, yet it was one he was in no position to photograph, for reasons both technical- and safety-related. But if his building could hold up and he could survive this, there would be plenty of damage to photograph all through Hangtree. Maybe even a few corpses, trampled and ruined. Oh, how he'd love to photograph those. It became something like a silent prayer in his mind as he watched the rumbling onslaught go by: God, let there be corpses!

As if in answer, he saw the remarkable and revolting sight of two men being carried along in the flow, impaled on the six-foot longhorn racks of two huge bulls. "Them Drunken Earhardt Brothers" had surely, given their alcoholic lifestyle, anticipated that they might likely reach the end of their days on some dusty street or alleyway, but surely neither had supposed those deaths would come on the stabbing and swaying horns of a massive surge of longhorn cattle stampeding through the streets of their town as the morning lightened around them.

Over at the Cattleman, Pedro Sanchez, finished with dumping grease, had turned his attention to chalk-writing the day's special on the blackboard sign that sat just by the front door.

Fresh Beef Newly Arrived—
Steaks Half-Priced
TODAY ONLY

Engrossed in his scribing, he did not look up until the thundering noise he seemed to be hearing, and the strange vibration of the ground, could not be ignored. Crouched before the sign, he turned his head, and time stopped.

"*Dulce madre de Dios!*" He leaped up and ducked inside the recessed entrance as a wall of living muscle powered past the building, hooves hammering the Texas dirt. An errant horn nicked at the sign he'd just chalked and sent it flying into the welter, where it was trampled into splinters.

Johnny Cross had seen many a sight in his day. Never anything like this.

Hangtree was being slammed by the biggest herd of stampeding cattle he had ever seen, or so it appeared to him. With everything in dust-blurred motion, it was difficult to gain perspective on just how big the herd really was. Whatever the answer to that question, the herd was stampeding with lethal force. From his perspective in an alley-way, where he had stopped for his morning bladder-draining, he saw something tumbling under the unending hoofbeats, and recognized an old dog that typically roamed up and down the street all day. A sad but fast ending for a harmless old beast.

A rider, moving along beside the herd, was suddenly pushed, on his horse, into the end of the alley where Cross was. The horse, terrified, had been trying hard, against its rider's guidance, to get out of and away from the stampede flow, and the alley had come up at just the right moment to let it do so. Johnny Cross watched the rider trying to calm and still the horse, recognized the man's face, and quietly drew his sidearm.

"Excuse me, Mr. Toleen," he hollered above the rumble. "Once you get that mount settled, why don't you get down off that saddle and let's you and me have a little talk about what the living hell is going on here?"

Drew Toleen finally got his panting, heaving horse under control, and looked at the man who had accosted him. He had the look of law about him, and Toleen didn't like it. He glared at Cross as he drew his pistol.

"I got no time for jawing with a law-dog," he said, and raised his weapon.

Johnny Cross put the bullet right into the space between Toleen's brows. The outlaw grunted and jerked, the horse backed up and bucked, and Toleen was thrown out into the stampede, where his corpse was trampled and rolled until Drew Toleen, who had shot his own brother to death and left his carcass beside the Hangtree Road, was little more than pulp wearing filthy, battered clothing.

"One more bad man gone," Cross muttered to himself. He refreshed the spent chamber and holstered the pistol, and wondered how it was that all this was happening, and why.

"And I thought it was going to be a quiet day," he muttered to himself.

Sam Heller discovered the stampede in much the same way Johnny Cross and most of the towns-folk did. He was heading for an early breakfast at that same little struggling café he occasionally visited because he liked seeing David competing with Goliath, the latter being the well-established Cattleman eatery.

He heard the rumble first, saw the cloud of dust moving toward town, then the lowing and bawling of cattle and the yells of men seemingly steering them along, as best an amazing conglomeration such as this one could be steered. Heller gaped and backed up against the wall of the nearest building, and moments later the herd flashed past him. If he'd stepped forward as much as a foot, he'd have been pulled under the hooves.

It was the fact that men were driving this stampede that revealed the most. These were the same cattle, quite surely, that had been rounded up and held in the vicinity of Resurrection Gulch. He recalled how he'd viewed the big herd and thought about that story out of East Texas about the robbery done there under the cover of a stampede.

Forget breakfast. He had to get to the bank.

It would be no easy task, considering the current circumstances in Hangtree. Which, he supposed, was exactly the intent of the bank robbers . . . assuming there were any.

One thing was sure: This wasn't being done for recreation. Something meaningful was happening here. Something was behind this.

Heller waited until the density of the stampede lessened. Gaps began to appear in the driving herd, not short enough to let him get across, not yet, anyway. He steadied and readied himself, waiting for the right moment.

The tip of a longhorn slashed across his right cheek, cutting it. He grunted in pain and pulled back, blood running down his face and under his collarless shirt. With his tongue he explored the inside of his jaw. No, the cut had not gone all the way through. Just a painful, bleeding furrow across his cheek.

A moment later the biggest gap he'd seen appeared, and with hardly a moment to think about it, he raced out into the street and across the open space. He barely made it before the next surge of cattle filled the gap and pursued the younger and faster cattle ahead of them. The mass of cattle was less dense here, stragglers and older beasts for the most part.

Sam saw his own brand on some of the cattle, and an idea came. A loco notion, but everything happening here today was loco. As another gap appeared, Sam picked out a particular old longhorn, one he actually thought he recognized. Seeing his own brand, seared in at an odd angle on this bovine, he was almost certain this was the longhorn that one of his hired drovers, lanky Bernard Silverman, would sometimes ride around the camp for comic effect. It was a slower cow than most of those that had passed, and Sam could see that it was near the end of the herd. Sam darted out to it and swung himself up on its back, leaning forward and holding to its horns. The beast didn't much like it, but being ridden was not new to it, thanks to the joker Silverman, so it made only feeble efforts to shake Heller off.

"Bossy," he said in the longhorn's ear, "take me to the bank, please. Fast as you can go." Then he hung on and rode, his unusual mount falling farther and farther behind.

Johnny Cross had worked his way around to the bank and ascertained what was going on. There was activity in there, and it was well before the bank's usual opening time. It all came together in his mind, and without hesitating he made a crouched dash for the back door.

From the vantage point she had attained on the balcony of the farrier's, Julia Canton should have been able to see Cross making his run toward the bank. She did not, though, because she was no longer where she had been. She was lying atop the rubble of the balcony, which had had its supports knocked from beneath it by errant stampeding cattle. It had gone down hard and fast, and in the process of falling with it, she had knocked her head hard against a plunging balcony rail. With her prior concussion still in the healing process, she had gone out cold at once, and only by good fortune and the fact that the rubble on which she lay made for a high enough stack that the cattle avoided it had she avoided being trampled.

She came to slowly, the stampede continuing but thinned greatly from what it had been when she fell. It was impossible to recall exactly what had happened, but she knew what she was seeing when her blurry eyes took in the sight of young

Angeline Caldwell sitting in the middle of the street, her leg oddly twisted. The child was sobbing pitifully.

Julia did not know exactly from where the girl had come, but her best supposition was that she had been at the bank with the robbers and had found an opportunity to flee. She must have been caught in the stampede, but been lucky enough to avoid being trampled. Trampled, at least, any more severely than to give her a leg injury.

If she remained out there, though, the next surge—and there was one coming that Julia could hear already—might well squash the little girl into the ground.

Julia rose and, despite finding herself quite dizzy, moved out into the street. She swept the crying little girl into her arms and made for the other side of the street, getting Angeline safely into a recessed corner doorway just as the new clump of racing cattle rumbled by. Not even realizing that her face was half-covered in blood running from her reopened head injury, she smiled at the girl she had rescued, and had a sense of well-being despite the dangerous circumstances . . .

. . . A sense of well-being that was still lingering when the top of a horn gouged into Julia's side and lifted her up and away, leaving the sobbing Angeline instantly alone. The horn cut deeply into Julia's innards, driving up inside her like a spike and rupturing several organs, including her heart. When at last Julia's body fell from the horn that held it, she knew nothing of it, and was

no longer present to feel her body being beaten
to jelly, bones shattering into splinters, ribs col-
lapsing, spine broken in multiple places.

The tombstone was the finest in the church
burial ground. No rough wooden marker this
one; Sam Heller had a fine stone marker made
and engraved. The plaque given to Julia by the
town the night before she died was inset into
the stone to perfection, leaving the young woman
forever memorialized not as the daughter of the
criminal she really was, but as *Julia Pepperday
Canton:* BRAVE MAIDEN OF HANGTREE.

While her battered corpse still lay in the street,
Otto Perkins had done his best to get a photograph of it in all its gore, but Sam Heller had
knocked him cold with the butt of his mule-leg
firearm and had her body carried away before
the meager little man could wake up.

In years to come, when the magic of the kind
of photography practiced by Otto Perkins had
evolved into moving pictures, many a Saturday
morning serial reel would feature one variation
or another of the way Sam Heller and others had
managed to stop the robbery at the last moment.

One of the others was Arvil Caldwell, who,
while the outlaws in the bank lobby were preoc-
cupied with watching the stampede passing the
windows, had gotten hold of a particularly well-
filled and therefore heavy bank strongbox. In it
was gold that was the possession of Sam Heller.

As Cale Pepperday was looking out of the open bank vault and realizing that his little girl hostage had managed to get away, Caldwell had slammed the heavy box hard against the side of Pepperday's head, nearly crushing it between the box and the vault door. Pepperday collapsed with a low moan, knocked senseless. He was thus spared some of the pain he would have felt had he been conscious when Caldwell carefully dragged him to just the right spot at the vault entrance to have his head crushed like a walnut when Caldwell closed the vault upon it.

It took the bank janitor almost a week to fully clean up the resulting bloody mess.

What had made it possible for Caldwell to kill the scoundrel so methodically was the fact that Johnny Cross had showed up at just the right moment and disarmed the robbers still in the lobby, men who should have paid more heed to their work than to the cattle passing outside.

In the later years of his long life, Timothy Holt would give up the work of sweeping, becoming instead the town's official guide at the Hangtree Church Burial Ground, where visitors for decades to come would to see the grave of the heroine out of Texas lore, Julia Canton, whose pulverized body lay beneath the sod and had long since become one with the soil of Hangtree, Texas.

J. A. Johnstone on William W. Johnstone
"When the Truth Becomes Legend"

William W. Johnstone was born in southern Missouri, the youngest of four children. He was raised with strong moral and family values by his minister father, and tutored by his schoolteacher mother. Despite this, he quit school at age fifteen.

"I have the highest respect for education," he says, "but such is the folly of youth, and wanting to see the world beyond the four walls and the blackboard."

True to this vow, Bill attempted to enlist in the French Foreign Legion ("I saw Gary Cooper in *Beau Geste* when I was a kid and I thought the French Foreign Legion would be fun") but was rejected, thankfully, for being underage. Instead, he joined a traveling carnival and did all kinds of odd jobs. It was listening to the veteran carny folk, some of whom had been on the circuit since the late 1800s, telling amazing tales about their experiences, which planted the storytelling seed in Bill's imagination.

"They were mostly honest people, despite the bad reputation traveling carny shows had back then," Bill remembers. "Of course, there were exceptions. There was one guy named Picky, who got that name because he was a master pickpocket. He could steal a man's socks right off his feet without him knowing. Believe me, Picky got us chased out of more than a few towns."

After a few months of this grueling existence, Bill returned home and finished high school. Next came stints as a deputy sheriff in the Tallulah, Louisiana, Sheriff's Department, followed by a hitch in the U.S. Army. Then he began a career in radio broadcasting at KTLD in Tallulah, which would last sixteen years. It was there that he fine-tuned his storytelling skills. He turned to writing in 1970, but it wouldn't be until 1979 that his first novel, *The Devil's Kiss,* was published. Thus began the full-time writing career of William W. Johnstone. He wrote horror (*The Uninvited*), thrillers (*The Last of the Dog Team*), even a romance novel or two. Then, in February 1983, *Out of the Ashes* was published. Searching for his missing family in the aftermath of a post-apocalyptic America, rebel mercenary and patriot Ben Raines is united with the civilians of the Resistance forces and moves to the forefront of a revolution for the nation's future.

Out of the Ashes was a smash. The series would continue for the next twenty years, winning Bill three generations of fans all over the world. The series was often imitated but never duplicated. "We all tried to copy the Ashes series," said one publishing executive, "but Bill's uncanny ability, both then and now, to predict in which direction the political winds were blowing brought a certain immediacy to the table no one else could capture." The Ashes series would end its run with more than thirty-four books and twenty million copies in print, making it one of the most successful men's action series in American book publishing. (The Ashes series also, Bill notes with a touch of pride, got him on the FBI's Watch List for its less than flattering portrayal of spineless politicians and the growing power of big government over our lives, among other things. In that respect, I often find myself saying, "Bill was years ahead of his time.")

Always steps ahead of the political curve, Bill's recent thrillers, written with myself, include *Vengeance Is Mine, Invasion USA, Border War, Jackknife, Remember the Alamo, Home Invasion, Phoenix Rising, The Blood of Patriots, The Bleeding Edge*, and the upcoming *Suicide Mission*.

It is with the western, though, that Bill found his greatest success and propelled him onto both the *USA Today* and the *New York Times* bestseller lists.

Bill's western series include *The Mountain Man, Matt Jensen, the Last Mountain Man, Preacher, The Family Jensen, Luke Jensen, Bounty Hunter, Eagles, MacCallister* (an Eagles spin-off), *Sidewinders, The Brothers O'Brien, Sixkiller, Blood Bond, The Last Gunfighter,* and the upcoming new series

Flintlock and *The Trail West.* Coming in May 2013 is the hardcover western *Butch Cassidy, The Lost Years.*

"The Western," Bill says, "is one of the few true art forms that is one hundred percent American. I liken the Western as America's version of England's Arthurian legends, like the Knights of the Round Table, or Robin Hood and his Merry Men. Starting with the 1902 publication of *The Virginian* by Owen Wister, and followed by the greats like Zane Grey, Max Brand, Ernest Haycox, and of course Louis L'Amour, the Western has helped to shape the cultural landscape of America.

"I'm no goggle-eyed college academic, so when my fans ask me why the Western is as popular now as it was a century ago, I don't offer a 200-page thesis. Instead, I can only offer this: The Western is honest. In this great country, which is suffering under the yoke of political correctness, the Western harks back to an era when justice was sure and swift. Steal a man's horse, rustle his cattle, rob a bank, a stagecoach, or a train, you were hunted down and fitted with a hangman's noose. One size fit all.

"Sure, we westerners are prone to a little embellishment and exaggeration and, I admit it, occasionally play a little fast and loose with the facts. But we do so for a very good reason—to enhance the enjoyment of readers.

"It was Owen Wister, in *The Virginian* who first coined the phrase *'When you call me that, smile.'* Legend has it that Wister actually heard those words spoken by a deputy sheriff in Medicine Bow, Wyoming, when another poker player called him a son-of-a-bitch.

"Did it really happen, or is it one of those myths that have passed down from one generation to the next? I honestly don't know. But there's a line in one of my favorite Westerns of all time, *The Man Who Shot Liberty Valance,* where the newspaper editor tells the young reporter, 'When the truth becomes legend, print the legend.'

"These are the words I live by."

Turn the page for an exciting preview!

*He is brave, tough as leather, takes no prisoners,
and has left behind a trail of deadly enemies—
outlaws he's hunted down or killed with
the cold heart of a man used to violence.
A feared bounty hunter and the scourge of bad men
everywhere, Flintlock carries an ancient Hawken
muzzle-loader, handed down to him from
the mountain man who raised him. He stands
as the towering hero of a new Johnstone saga.*

FLINTLOCK

Busted out of prison by an outlaw friend,
Flintlock joins a hunt for a fortune—a golden
bell hanging in a remote monastery.
But between the smoldering ruin of his former
jail cell and a treasure in the Arizona mountains
there will be blood at a U.S. Army fort,
a horrifying brush with Apache warriors,
and a dozen wild adventures with the schemers,
shootists, madmen, and lost women who find
their way to Flintlock's side. From a vicious,
superstitious half-breed to the great Geronimo
himself, Flintlock meets the frontier's
most murderous hardcases—many whom
he must find a way to kill . . .

FLINTLOCK

by William W. Johnstone
with J. A. Johnstone

On sale now wherever Pinnacle Books are sold.
Visit us at www.kensingtonbooks.com.

CHAPTER ONE

"I'm gonna hang you tomorrow at sunup, Sam Flintlock, an' I can't guarantee to break your damned neck on account of how I never hung anybody afore," the sheriff said. "I'll try, lay to that, but you see how it is with me."

"The hammering stopped about an hour ago, so I figured my time was near," Flintlock said.

"A real nice gallows, you'll like it," Sheriff Dave Cobb said. "An' I'll make sure it's hung with red, white and blue bunting so you can go out in style. You'll draw a crowd, Sam. If'n that makes you feel better."

"This pissant town railroaded me into a noose, Cobb. You know it and I know it," Flintlock said.

"Damnit, boy, you done kilt Smilin' Dan Sedly and just about everybody in this valley was kissin' kin o' his. Ol' Dan was a well-liked man."

"He was wanted by the law for bank robbery and murder," Flintlock said.

"Not in this town he wasn't," Cobb said.

The sheriff was a middle-aged man and inclined to be jolly by times. He was big in the belly and a black, spade-shaped beard spread over the lapels of a broadcloth suit coat that looked to be half as old as he was.

"No hard feelings, huh, Sam?" he said. "I mean about the hangin' an' all. Like I told you, I'll do my best. I've been reading a book about how to set the noose an' sich an' I reckon I'll get it right."

"I got no beef against you, Cobb," Flintlock said. "You're the town lawman and you've got a job to do."

"How old are you, young feller?" the lawman said.

"Forty. I guess."

"Still too young to die." Cobb sighed. "Ah well, tell you what, I'll bring you something nice for your last meal tonight. How about steak and eggs? You like steak and eggs?"

"I don't much care, Sheriff, but there's one thing you can do for me."

"Just ask fer it. I'm a giving, generous man. Dave Cobb by name, Dave Cobb by nature, I always say."

"Let me have my grandpappy's old Hawken rifle," Flintlock said. "It will be a comfort to me."

Doubt showed in Cobb's face. "Now, I don't know about that. That's agin all the rules."

"Hell, Cobb, the Hawken hasn't been shot in thirty, forty years," Flintlock said. "I ain't much likely to use it to bust out of jail."

"You're a strange one, Sam Flintlock," the lawman said. "Why did you carry that old gun around anyhow?"

"Call me sentimental, Cobb. It was left to me as a legacy, like."

"See, my problem is, Sam, you could use that old long gun as a club. Bash my brains out when I wasn't lookin'."

"Not that rifle, I won't. Your head is too thick, Sheriff. I might damage the stock."

Cobb thought for a while, his shaggy black eyebrows beetling. Finally he smiled and said, "All right, I'll bring it to you. But I see you making any fancy moves with that old Hawken, I'll shoot your legs off so you can still live long enough to be hung. You catch my drift?"

"You have my word, Sheriff, I won't give you any trouble."

Cobb nodded. "Well, you're a personable enough feller, even though you ain't so well set up an' all, so I'll take you at your word."

"I appreciate it," Flintlock said. "See, I'm named for that Hawken."

"Your real name Hawken, like?"

"No. My grandpappy named me for a flintlock rifle, seeing as how I never knew my pa's name."

"Hell, why didn't he give you his own name, that grandpa of yourn?"

"He said every man should have his father's name. He told me he'd call me Flintlock after the Hawken until I found my ma and she told me who my pa was and what he was called."

"You ever find her?"

"No. I never did, but I'm still on the hunt for her. Or at least I was."

"Your grandpa was a mountain man?"

"Yeah, he was with Bridger an' Hugh Glass an' them, at least for a spell. Then he helped survey the Platte and the Sweetwater with Kit Carson and Fremont."

"Strange, restless breed they were, mountain men."

"You could say that."

"I'll bring you the Hawken, but mind what I told you, about shootin' off a part of yourself."

"I ain't likely to forget," Flintlock said.

CHAPTER TWO

"Pssst . . ."

Sam Flintlock sat up on his cot, his mind cobwebbed by sleep.

"Pssst . . ."

What was that? Rats in the corners again?

"Hell, look up here, stupid."

Flintlock rose to his feet. There was a small barred window high on the wall of his cell where a bearded face looked down at him.

"I see you're prospering, Sammy," the man said, grinning. "Settin' all nice and cozy in the town hoosegow."

Flintlock scowled. "Come to watch me hang, Abe?"

"Nah, I was just passin' through when I saw the gallows," Abe Roper said. "I asked who was gettin' hung and they said a feller with a big bird tattooed on his throat that goes by the name of Sam Flintlock. I knew it had to be you. There ain't another ranny in the West with a big bird an' that handle."

"Here to gloat, Abe?" Flintlock said. "Gettin' even for old times?"

"Hell, no, I got nothing agin you, Sam. You got me two years in Yuma but you treated me fair and square. An' you gave my old lady money the whole time I was inside. Now why did you do a dumb thing like that?"

"You had growing young 'uns. Them kids had to be fed and clothed."

"Yeah, but why the hell did you do it?"

"I just told you."

"I got no liking for bounty hunters, Sammy, but you was a true-blue white man, taking care of my family like that." Roper was silent for a moment, then said, "Sally and the kids passed about three years ago from the cholera."

"I'm sorry to hear that," Flintlock said. "I can close my eyes and still see their faces."

"It was a hurtful thing, Sam, and me being away on the scout at the time."

"You gonna stick around for the hanging, Abe?" Flintlock said.

"Hell, no, and neither are you."

"What do you mean?"

"I mean there's a barrel of gunpowder against this wall and it's due to go up in"—Roper looked down briefly—"oh, I'd say less than half a minute."

The man waved a quick hand. "Hell, I got to light a shuck."

Flintlock stood rooted to the spot for a moment.

Then he yelled a startled curse at Roper, grabbed the rifle off his cot and pulled the mattress on top of him.

A couple of seconds later the Mason City jail blew up with such force its shingle roof soared into the air and landed intact twenty yards away on top of the brand-new gallows. The jail roof and the gallows collapsed in a cloud of dust and killed Sheriff Cobb's pregnant sow that had been wallowing in the mud under the platform.

A shattering shower of adobe and splintered wood rained down on Flintlock and acrid dust filled his lungs. He threw the mattress aside and staggered to his feet, just as Abe Roper kicked aside debris and stepped through the hole in the jailhouse wall.

"Sam, get the hell out of there," Roper said. "I got your hoss outside."

Flintlock grabbed the Hawken, none the worse for wear, and stumbled outside.

As Roper swung into the saddle, Chinese Charlie Fong, grinning as always, tossed Flintlock the reins of a paint.

"Good to see you again, Sammy," Fong said.

"Feeling's mutual, Charlie," Flintlock said.

He mounted quickly and ate Roper's dust as he followed the outlaw out of town at a canter.

Roper turned in the saddle. "Crackerjack bang, Sammy, huh? Have you ever seen the like?"

"Son of a gun, you could've killed me," Flintlock said.

"So what? Who the hell would miss ya?" Roper said.

"Somebody's gonna miss this paint pony I'm riding," Flintlock said.

"Hell, yeah, it's the sheriff's hoss," Roper grinned. "Better than the ten-dollar mustang you rode in on, Sam."

"Damn you, Abe, Cobb's gonna hang me, then hang me all over again for hoss theft," Flintlock said.

"Well, he'll have to catch you first," Roper said, kicking his mount into a gallop.

After an hour of riding through the southern foothills of the Chuska Mountains, the massive rampart of red sandstone buttes and peaks that runs north all the way to the Utah border, Roper drew rein and he and Flintlock waited until Charlie Fong caught up.

"Where are we headed, Abe?" Flintlock said. "I hope you've got a good hideout all picked out."

He and Roper were holed up in a stand of mixed juniper and piñon. A nearby high meadow was thick with yellow bells and wild strawberry, and the waning afternoon air smelled sweet of pine and wildflowers.

"We're headed for Fort Defiance, up in the old Navajo country. It's been abandoned for years but the army's moved back, temporary-like, until ol' Geronimo is either penned up or dead."

Flintlock scratched at a bug bite under his

buckskin shirt and said, "Is that wise, me riding into an army fort when I'm on the scout?"

"There ain't no fightin' sodjers there, Sammy, just cooks an' quartermasters an' the like," Roper said. "All the cavalry is out, lookin' fer Geronimo an' them."

"We gonna stay in an army barracks?" Flint-lock said. "Say it ain't so."

"Nah, me an' Charlie got us a cabin near the officers' quarters, a cozy enough berth if you're not a complainin' man."

Roper peered hard at Flintlock's rugged, un-shaven face and then his throat. "Damnit, Sam, I never did get used to looking at that big bird, even when we rode together."

"I was raised rough," Flintlock said. "You know that."

"Old Barnabas do that to you?" Roper said, passing the makings.

"He wanted it done, but when I was twelve he got an Assiniboine woman to do the tattooing. As I recollect, it hurt considerable."

"What the hell is it? Some kind of eagle?"

Flintlock built his cigarette and Roper gave him a match. "It's a thunderbird." He thumbed the match into flame and lit his cigarette. "Barn-abas wanted a black and red thunderbird, on account of how the Indians reckon it's a sacred bird."

"He wanted it that big? Hell, it pretty much covers your neck and down into your chest."

"Barnabas said folks would remember me

because of the bird. He told me that a man folks don't remember is of no account."

"He was a hard old man, was Barnabas, him and them other mountain men he hung with. A tough, mean bunch as ever was."

"They taught me," Flintlock said. "Each one of them taught me something."

"Like what, for instance?"

"They taught me about whores and whiskey and how to tell the good ones from the bad. They taught me how to stalk a man and how to kill him. And they taught me to never answer a bunch of damned fool questions."

Roper laughed. "Sounds like old Barnabas and his pals all right."

"One more thing, Abe. You saved my life today, and they taught me to never forget a thing like that."

Roper, smiling, watched a hawk in flight against the dark blue sky, then again directed his attention to Flintlock.

"You ever heard of the Golden Bell of Santa Elena, Sam?" he said.

"Can't say as I have."

"You will. And after I tell you about it, I'll ask you to repay the favor you owe me."

CHAPTER THREE

"Are you sure you saw deer out here, Captain Shaw? It might have been a shadow among the trees."

"Look at the tracks in the wash, Major. Deer have passed this way and not long ago."

"I see tracks all right," Major Philip Ashton said. He looked around him. "But I'm damned if I see any deer."

"Sir, may I suggest we move farther up the wash as far as the foothills," Captain Owen Shaw said. "Going on dusk the deer will move out of the timber."

Ashton, a small, compact man with a florid face, an affable disposition and a taste for bonded whiskey, nodded. "As good a suggestion as any, Captain. We'll wait until dark and if we don't see a deer we'll leave it for another day."

"As you say, sir," Shaw said.

He watched the major walk ahead of him. Like himself, Ashton wore civilian clothes but he carried a regulation Model 1873 Trapdoor Springfield rifle. Shaw was armed with a .44-40 Winchester because he wanted nothing to go wrong on this venture, no awkward questions to be answered later.

Major Ashton, who had never held a combat command, carried his rifle at the slant, as though advancing on an entrenched enemy and not a herd of nonexistent mule deer.

Shaw was thirty years old that spring. He'd served in a frontier cavalry regiment, but he'd been banished to Fort Defiance as a commissary officer after a passionate, though reckless, affair with the young wife of a farrier sergeant.

Shaw wasn't at all troubled by his exile. It was safer to dole out biscuit and salt beef than do battle with Sioux and Cheyenne warriors.

Of course, the Apaches were a problem, but since the Navajo attacked the fort in 1858 and 1860 and both times were badly mauled, it seemed that the wily Geronimo was giving the place a wide berth.

That last suited Captain Shaw perfectly. He had big plans and they sure as hell didn't involve Apaches.

The wash, dry now that the spring melt was over, made a sharp cut to the north and the two officers followed it through a grove of stunted juniper and willow onto a rocky plateau bordered by thick stands of pine.

In the distance the fading day painted the Chuska peaks with wedges of deep lilac shadow and out among the foothills coyotes yipped. The jade sky was streaked with banners of scarlet and gold, the streaming colors of the advancing night.

Major Ashton walked onto the plateau, his attention directed at the pines. His rifle at the ready, he stopped and scanned the trees with his field glasses.

Without turning his head, he said, "Nothing moving yet, Captain."

Shaw made no answer.

"You have a buck spotted?" the major whispered.

Again, he got no reply.

Ashton turned.

Shaw's rifle was pointed right at his chest.

"What in blazes are you doing, Captain Shaw?" Ashton said, his face alarmed.

"Killing you, Major."

Owen Shaw fired.

The soft-nosed .44-40 round tore into the major's chest and plowed through his lungs. Even as the echoing report of the Winchester racketed around the plateau, Ashton fell to his hands and knees and coughed up a bouquet of glistening red blossoms.

Shaw smiled and shot Ashton again, this time in the head. The major fell on his side and all the life that remained in him fled.

Moving quickly, Shaw stood over Ashton and fired half a dozen shots into the air, the spent cartridge cases falling on and around the major's body. He then pulled a Smith & Wesson .32 from the pocket of his tweed hunting jacket, placed the muzzle against his left thigh and pulled the trigger.

A red-hot poker of pain burned across Shaw's leg, but when he looked down at the wound he was pleased. It was only a flesh wound but it was bleeding nicely, enough to make him look a hero when he rode into Fort Defiance.

Limping slightly, Shaw retraced his steps along the dry wash to the place where he and Ashton had tethered their horses. He looked behind him and to his joy saw that he'd left a blood trail. Good! There was always the possibility that a cavalry patrol had returned to the fort and their Pima scouts could be bad news. The blood would help his cover-up.

He gathered up the reins of the major's horse and swung into the saddle. There was no real need to hurry but he forced his horse into a canter, Ashton's mount dragging on him.

It was an officer's duty to recover the body of a slain comrade, but Ashton had been of little account and not well liked. When Shaw told of the Apache ambush and his desperate battle to save the wounded major, that little detail would be overlooked.

And his own bloody wound spoke loud of gallantry and devotion to duty.

Lamps were already lit when Captain Owen Shaw rode into Fort Defiance, a sprawling complex of buildings, some of them ruins, grouped around a dusty parade ground.

He staged his entrance well.

Not for him to enter at a gallop and hysterically warn of Apaches, rather he slumped in the saddle and kept his horse to a walk . . . the wounded warrior's noble return.

He was glad that just as he rode past the sutler's store, big, laughing Sergeant Patrick Tone stepped outside, a bottle of whiskey tucked under his arm.

"Sergeant," Shaw said, making sure he sounded exhausted and sore hurt, "sound officer's call. Direct the gentlemen to the commandant's office."

"Where is Major Ashton, sir?" Tone said, his Irish brogue heavy on his tongue. Like many soldiers in the Indian-fighting army, he'd been born and bred in the Emerald Isle and was far from the rainy green hills of his native land.

"He's dead. Apaches. Now carry out my order."

Tone shifted the bottle from his right to his left underarm and snapped off a salute. Then he stepped quickly toward the enlisted men's barracks, roaring for the bugler.

Shaw dismounted outside the administration building, a single-story adobe structure, its timber porch hung with several large clay ollas that held drinking water. The ollas' constant evaporation supposedly helped keep the interior offices cool, a claim the soldiers vehemently denied.

After leaning against his horse for a few moments, the action of an exhausted man, Shaw limped up the three steps to the porch, drops of blood from his leg starring the rough pine.

He stopped, swaying slightly, when he saw a woman bustling toward him across the parade ground, her swirling skirts lifting veils of yellow dust.

Shaw smiled inwardly. This was getting better and better. Here comes the distraught widow.

Maude Ashton, the major's wife, was a plump, motherly woman with a sweet, heart-shaped face that normally wore a smile. But now she looked concerned, as though she feared to hear news she already knew would be bad.

Maude mounted the steps and one look at the expression on Shaw's face and the blood on his leg told her all she needed to know. She asked the question anyway. "Captain Shaw, where is my husband?"

As the stirring notes of officer's call rang around him, Shaw made an act of battling back a sob. "Oh, Maude . . ."

He couldn't go on.

The captain opened his arms wide, tears staining his cheeks, and Maude Ashton ran between them. Shaw clasped her tightly and whispered, "Philip is dead."

Maude had been a soldier's wife long enough to know that the day might come when she'd have to face those three words. Now she repeated them. "Philip is dead . . ."

"Apaches," Shaw said. He steadied himself and

managed, "They jumped us out by Rock Wash and Major Ashton fell in the first volley."

Maude took a step back. Her pretty face, unstained by tears, was stony. "And Philip is still out there?"

Boots thudded onto the porch and Shaw decided to wait until his two officers were present before he answered Maude's irritating question.

First Lieutenant Frank Hedley was in his early fifties, missing the left arm he'd lost at Gettysburg as a brevet brigadier general of artillery. He was a private, withdrawn man, too fond of the bottle to be deemed fit for further promotion. He'd spent the past fifteen years in the same regular army rank. This had made him bitter and his drinking and irascible manner worsened day by day.

Standing next to him was Second Lieutenant Miles Howard, an earnest nineteen-year-old fresh out of West Point. His application for a transfer to the hard-riding 5th Cavalry had recently been approved on the recommendation of the Point's superintendent, the gallant Colonel Wesley Merritt, the regiment's former commander.

Howard had a romantic view of the frontier war, his imagination aflame with flying banners, bugle calls and thundering charges with the saber. He'd never fought Apaches.

"Where is the major?" Hedley said.

"He's dead," Shaw said. "We got hit by Apaches at Rock Wash and Major Ashton fell."

Hedley turned and saw the dead officer's horse. "Where is he?"

Shaw shook his head and then stared directly and sincerely at Maude. "I had to leave him. The Apaches wanted his body but I stood over him and drove them away. But I was sore wounded and could not muster the strength to lift the gallant major onto his horse."

Lieutenant Howard, more perceptive and more sympathetic than Hedley, watched blood drops from Shaw's leg tick onto the timber.

"Sir, you need the post surgeon," he said.

"Later, Lieutenant. Right now I want you and Mr. Hedley in the commandant's office," Shaw said, grimacing, a badly wounded soldier determined to be brave.